**Anonymous**

# The Horse: His Care and Treatment, From English and French Authority

Anatiposi

**Anonymous**

# The Horse: His Care and Treatment, From English and French Authority

Reprint of the original, first published in 1872.

1st Edition 2023   |   ISBN: 978-3-38212-976-7

Anatiposi Verlag is an imprint of Outlook Verlagsgesellschaft mbH.

Verlag (Publisher): Outlook Verlag GmbH, Zeilweg 44, 60439 Frankfurt, Deutschland
Vertretungsberechtigt (Authorized to represent): E. Roepke, Zeilweg 44, 60439 Frankfurt, Deutschland
Druck (Print): Books on Demand GmbH, In de Tarpen 42, 22848 Norderstedt, Deutschland

# THE HORSE:

## HIS CARE AND TREATMENT,

FROM ENGLISH AND FRENCH AUTHORITY.

CONTAINING INSTRUCTIONS IN

*PURCHASING, CARE OF, RIDING, TRAINING, ALL THE TRICKS OF DEALERS WHEN SELLING AND BUYING.*

THE RECIPES GIVEN IN THIS WORK ARE THE MOST VALUABLE THAT CAN BE OBTAINED.

ALSO,

VALUABLE INFORMATION CONCERNING OTHER DOMESTIC ANIMALS.

———

BOSTON:
CLARKSON & CO., PUBLISHERS.
1872.

Printed by

ALFRED MUDGE & SON, 34 School St., Boston.

# THE HORSE.

GOOD MEN, GOOD HORSES. — A horse is never vicious or intractable without a direct cause. If a horse is restive or timorous, you may be sure that these faults arise from defects in his education. He has been treated either awkardly or brutally. Commence the education of a horse at his birth; accustom him to the presence, voice and sight of man; speak and act gently; caress him, and do not startle him. All chastisement or cruelty confuses the animal and makes him wild. They are good men who make good horses.

HORSES, HOW TO JUDGE AND SELECT. —*Color.* — Light sorrel or chestnut, with feet, legs, and face white, are marks of kindness. A deep bay, with no white hair, will be a horse of great bottom, but a fool, especially if his face is a little dished. They are always tricky and unsafe. A black horse cannot stand the heat, nor a white one the cold. The more white about the head the greater his docility and gentleness. *Eye.* — If broad and full between the eyes, he may be depended on as a horse for being trained to anything. *Ears.* — Intelligent animals prick up their ears when spoken to; vicious ones threw their ears back. *Face and Neck.* — Dished-faced horses must always be avoided, and a broad forehead, high between the ears, indicates a very vicious disposition; while a long thin neck indicates a good disposition; contrawise, if short and thick; the nostrils of a good horse should be large.

HORSE, POINTS OF A GOOD. — He should be about fifteen and a half hands high; the head light and clean made; wide between the nostrils, and the nostrils themselves large, transparent and open; broad in the forehead; eyes prominent, clear and sparkling; ears small and neatly set on; neck rather short, and well set up; large arm or shoulder, well thrown back, and high; withers arched and high; legs fine, flat, thin and small-boned; body round and rather light, though sufficiently large to afford substance when it is needed; full chest, affording play for the lungs; back short, with the hind-quarters set on rather obliquely. Any one possessing a horse of this make and appearance, and weighing 1,100 or 1,200 pounds, may rest assured he has a horse of all work, and a bargain well worth getting hold of.

A well-shaped head, rather large; a long clean ear, full eye, neck rather long, but not too much arched; strong withers, lying well forward to catch the collar at the proper angle for draught, and broad shoulders well spread into the back; back very straight, ribs long and well rounded, hind legs bent at the hock, forelegs forward, hind-quarters somewhat round, but not sufficiently so to make them look short; the main and tail of strong, but not coarse hair, and with a fetlock about two inches long; broad knees, long hocks, short shanks, and hard ankles or fetlock joints, and round hoofs, well opened behind; and the nearer you can approach this description, the nearer the horse will be to perfection.

HOOF-QUARTER, CRACKED. — Many plans have been devised by which to heal a quarter crack — such as scoring with a knife, blistering, cutting with a sharp, hot iron, riveting and the like, all which, in many cases, have proved a failure. If the following directions are adopted, the fore feet will be sound in three months. Above the crack, and next to the hair, cut with your knife an incision half an inch long, crosswise of the crack, and about one quarter of an inch deep. Now from the incision draw a line one quarter of an inch each side, parallel with the crack, down to the shoe; then with your knife follow those lines, and cut through the enamel or crust of the foot. Now there is a piece of the crust to be taken out. This is done by loosening the top of the piece next to the hair with your knife, then with your forceps take hold of the piece and pull it off; that leaves a space of half an inch of the crust taken out from the hair down to the shoe. Fill the cavity with tar, and lace on a soft piece of leather to keep the tar in its place.

Keep the animal quiet for three or four days, and he is ready to drive, but it is best not to use him until the foot is perfectly sound. Shoe with a bar shoe, leaving some spring to the heel, so it will not. bear hard upon the weak quarter, and in three months you will have a sound foot.

HORSES, AGE OF BY TEETH. — A horse has forty teeth — twenty-four double teeth, or grinders, four tushes, or single file teeth, and twelve front teeth, called gatherers. As a general thing, mares have no tushes. Between two and three years old, the colt sheds his four middle teeth — two above and two below. After three years old two other teeth are shed, one on each side of those formerly changed; he now has eight colt's teeth and eight horse's teeth; when four years of age he cuts four new teeth. At five years of age the horse sheds his remaining colt's teeth, four in number, when his tushes appear. At six years of age his tushes are up, appearing white, small and sharp, while a small circle of young growing teeth is observable. The mouth is now complete. At eight years of age the teeth have filled up, the horse is aged, and his mouth is said to be full. *By Eyelid.* — After a horse is nine years old, a wrinkle comes on the eyelid, at the upper corner of the lower lid, and every year thereafter he has one well-defined wrinkle for each year over nine. If, for instance, a horse has three of these wrinkles, he is twelve; if four, he is thirteen. Add the number of wrinkles to nine, and you will invariably judge correctly of a horse's age.

HORSE'S EYES, TO TEST A. — To test a horse's eyes, look at the eye carefully, when the horse is in rather a dark stable. Note the shape and size of the pupil carefully, carry this in your mind while you turn your horse about to a strong light. If the pupil contracts and appears much smaller than in the first instance, you may infer that the horse has a good strong eye; but if the pupil remains nearly of the same size in both cases, his eyes are weak, and you had better have nothing to do with him.

HORSE, TO BREAK OF PAWING — Nail iron strips across the horse's stall — say strips one inch wide and one-half inch thick, six inches apart, securely nailed crossways his stall — and they will soon make him sick of pawing, when he will no doubt find some other way of passing away the time. If he takes to kicking, fasten the trace chain around his fetlock; if to cribbing, trade him off and let some one else cure him of that detestable habit.

HORSE-COLLARS AND SADDLES, ETC., WOODEN. — Galled shoulders and backs are to no small extent due to the soft pads and cushions which are pressed upon the tender skin under which the muscles play, and upon which great weight or draught is borne. The skin thickens and gets tough to some extent, but the softer or more padded the collar or saddle, the more liable is the skin to blister and gall. This is because the perspiration is retained, the skin softened and bone beneath. Horses whose backs galled under padded saddles would get well when used with well-fitting army saddles, which were simply hard wooden trees covered with rawhide, dry and hard, almost like iron. Why the hint has not been before taken we cannot imagine, but only recently have we seen wooden horse-collars introduced. They have been used for some time at the South — more, we fancy, from necessity than from choice, but with the best results. Now, two companies are manufacturing them in this city, and other hard materials not liable to absorb water are being introduced. Some are made to be used with hames; others have hooks or other attachment places for traces upon the collar itself. One patented material called " Flaxhorn " is very tough, capable of being worked into very light strong collars, saddle-trees, harnesses, saddles, and pads.

A wooden collar for ordinary work can be made which opens like ordinary hames, at the top, but the two parts are fastened together at the bottom by a strong iron hinge. Others open to go over the head of the horse at two points a little below the trace-hooks on each side; others still, chiefly in use for mules, we believe, do not open at all, but are made in one piece, with two spots cut out on each side, so that the collar will go over the head, and not hurt the bony projections over the eyes. As we see it, there is a great future for hard horse-collars, etc., and we fully believe they will be not only lighter, but far easier for horses than the heavy costly padded things they are now tortured with.

HORSES, WHEN UNSOUND. — Any of the following defects constitute unsoundness in a horse: —

Lameness of all kinds and degrees. Diseases of any of the internal organs. Cough of every kind, as long as it exists. Colds or catarrhs, while they last. Roaring, broken wind, thick wind, grese, mange, farcy and glanders; megrims or staggers, founder, convex feet, contracted feet, spavins and ringbones, enlargement of the sinews or ligaments, cataracts and other defects of the eyes, impairing sight.

The following may or may not occasion unsoundness, according to the state or degree in which they exist: Corns, splints, thrushes, bog-spavins, through pins, wind-galls, crib-biting. Curbs are unsoundness unless the horse has worked with them for some months without inconvenience.

Cutting, particularly speedy cutting, constitutes unsoundness when it cannot be remedied by care and skill. Quidding, when a confirmed habit, injures the soundness of a horse.

Defects, called blemishes, are: Scars from broken knees; capped hocks, splints, bog-spavins, and through pins; loss of hair from blisters or scars, enlargements from blows or cutting, and also specks or streaks on the corner of the eye.

Vices are: Restiveness, shying, bolting, running away, kicking, rearing, weaving, or moving the head from side to side, stringhalt, quidding, slipping the halter.

HORSES, CARE OF. — The man having the care of horses should be the embodiment of patience. His temper should always be under perfect control. He should never inflict any unnecessary pain, for it is only by the law of kindness that a horse can be trained and managed. No man ever yet struck a horse, but that he made the horse the worse for it. Patience and kindness will accomplish in every instance what whipping will fail to do. Horses having a vicious disposition are invariably made so from cruel treatment.

Horses are designed to work, and daily labor for them is as much a necessity to their existence as to that of man's. It is not the hard drawing and ponderous loads that wear out horses, and make them poor, baulky and worthless; but it is the hard driving, the worry by rough and inhuman drivers, that uses up more horse flesh, fat and muscle than all the labor a team performs. Another great reason why there are so few really sound animals, is because of their being put to work so soon. Horses are not developed until they are five, six or seven years old, and they should do very little work until they reach that period.

When a horse is worked hard its food should chiefly be oats; if not worked hard, its food should chiefly be hay; because oats supply more nourishment and flesh-making material than any other kind of food; hay not so much.

HORSES, FOOD FOR. — It is not possible to state the exact quantity of food a horse requires to keep him in good working condition. In all cases the horse himself tells whether he is getting too much or too little. The best feed for ordinary horses is hay and oats. Ten pounds of hay is a fair allowance of good hay, and to fast-working horses, from fifteen, twenty, or twenty-five pounds of oats; one-third of the hay may be given during the day, the balance at night. Horses differ so much in the quantity of hay they may eat without inconvenience in fact, they vary so much in size, age, breeding, temper, condition, and labor they are called upon to perform, that it is impossible to fix upon any specific rules for feeding them.

Oats should be bruised for an old horse, but not for a young one, because the former, through age and defective teeth, cannot chew them properly; the young horse can do so, and they are thus properly mixed with the saliva and turned into wholesome nutriment. Carrots given occasionally will give a fine, silky appearance to the coat, and experiments have shown that the best way to feed carrots is to give them with oats. If you are in the habit of feeding four quarts of oats to a mess, give two of oats and two of sliced carrots, and the result will be more satisfactory than if each were fed separately. Youatt writes of the carrot: " This root is held in much esteem. There is none better, nor perhaps so good; when first given it is slightly diuretic and laxative; but as the horse becomes accustomed to it these effects cease to be produced. They improve the state of the skin.

They form a good substitute for grass, and an excellent alterative for horses out of condition. To sick and idle horses they render grain unnecessary. They are beneficial in all chronic diseases connected with breathing, and have a marked influence upon chronic cough and broken wind. They are serviceable in diseases of the skin, and, in combination with oats, they restore a worn horse more than oats alone. It is also advantageous to chop hay fed to a horse, and to sprinkle the hay with water that has salt dissolved in it — a teaspoonful of salt to a bucket of water is sufficient. Rack-feeding is wasteful. The better plan is to feed with hay (chopped) from a manger, because the feed is not then thrown about, and is more easy to chew and digest.

As often as once a week a change of food should be made — one feed of cut hay and meal, or cut hay with shorts will do. Musty hay on no account should be fed to horses. Let the food be the best of its kind, for in the end it is the cheapest.

HORSES, WATER FOR. — In summer, when the horse sweats much, he should have water four or five times a day; under ordinary circumstances, two rules will guide the attendant. The first is, never to let the horse get very thirsty; the second, to give him water so often and in such quantity that he will not care to take any within an hour of going to fast work. The quantity of water which a horse will drink in twenty-four hours is uncertain; it varies so much that one will drink quite as much as other two or three. It is influenced by the food, the work, the weather, and the number of services; the demand for water also increases with the perspiration. Horses at fast work, and kept in hot stables, need a large allowance, which must be still larger in hot weather; horses of slow work may be permitted to take what quantity they please; but to those of fast work occasional restriction is necessary. Restriction is always necessary before fast work. A few quarts given an hour before going to work ought to suffice. Water should always be given before rather than after grain. Water your horses from a pond or stream rather than from a spring or well, because the latter is generally hard and cold, while the former is soft and comparatively warm. The horse prefers soft, muddy water to hard water, though ever so clear.

HORSE-FEEDING ON THE ROAD. — Many persons, in travelling, feed their horses too much and too often, continually stuffing them, and not allowing them time to rest and digest their food; of course they suffer from over-fulness and carrying unnecessary weight. Horses should be well fed in the evening, and must not be stuffed too full in the morning, and the travelling should be moderate on starting when the horse has a full stomach. If a horse starts in good condition, he can go twenty or twenty-five miles without feeding.

HORSES, CLEANING. — When brought in from work, warm with exertion, the horse must be rubbed down and then blanketed; but we would not blanket a horse in a good stable, as a general rule, except in extremely cold weather. A sharp-toothed curry-comb is the dread of a fine-skinned horse, and the brush and straw wisp answer the same purpose much better, if used as frequently as they should be. Mud should not be allowed to dry on the legs of a horse; it is the cause of half the swelled legs, scratches, and other affections of the feet with which they are afflicted.

HORSES, STABLES FOR. — The floor of the stable should be level, or nearly so. When it is inclined it causes the horse to hang back, because the incline causes his loins and hind parts to ache intolerably, and he hangs back in order, if possible, to get his hind legs beyond the gutter, thus diminishing, by many degrees, his standing up hill. The best bedding is that of straw, fine shavings from a planing mill, or sawdust — pine sawdust being best, and oak sawdust the worst. They should be allowed to stand on the naked floor as little as possible. "If I were asked," said a noted stock-raiser, "to account for my horses' legs and feet being in better order than those of my neighbor, I should attribute it to the four following circumstances : First, they are all shod with a few nails, so placed in the shoe as to per-mit the foot to expand every time they move. Second, that they all live in boxes, instead of stalls, and can move whenever they please. Third, they spend two hours daily in walking exercise when they are not at work. Fourth, that I have not a head-stall or trace-chain in my stable. These four circumstances comprehend the whole mystery of keeping horses' legs fine, and their feet in a sound working condition up to an old age.

HORSE STABLES, TO DEODORIZE. — Sawdust, wetted with sulphuric acid, diluted with forty parts of water, and distributed about horse stables, will remove the disagreeable ammonical smell, the sulphuric acid combining with the ammonia to form a salt. Chloride of lime slowly evolves chlorine, which will do the same thing, but then the chlorine smells worse than the am-monia. Sulphuric acid, on the contrary, is perfectly inodorous. The mixture must be kept in shallow earthenware vessels. The sulphuric acid used alone, either diluted or strong, would absorb more or less of the ammonia; and besides this, the saw-dust offers a large surface to the floating gas.

**HORSES, BLANKETING.** — In reference to blanketing horses in winter, it is doubtless true that blanketing keeps a horse's coat smoother in winter, and hence fine carriage horses and saddle horses will continue to be blanketed. But where horses are kept more for service than for show, we think they had better dispense with the blanket. Keeping them constantly covered makes them tender and liable to take cold. It is better to give them a warm stable, and plenty of straw for bedding, and good food. When they are to stand for any length of time out-of-doors in a cold winter's day, they should have blankets. And so when they come in from work steaming hot, they should be allowed to stand a short time until they have partially cooled off; then the blankets should be put on for an hour. Be careful and not delay putting on the blanket until they have become chilled.

**HORSES, POOR, HOW TO FATTEN.** — Many good horses devour large quantities of hay and grain, and still continue thin and poor. The food eaten is not properly assimilated. If the usual feed has been unground grain and hay, nothing but a change will effect any desirable alteration in the appearance of the animal. In case oil meal cannot be obtained readily, mingle a bushel of flaxseed with a bushel of barley, one of oats, and another bushel of Indian corn, and let it be ground into fine meal. This will be a fair proportion for all his feed. Or the meal or barley, oats and corn, in equal quantities, may at first be procured, and one-fourth of oil cake mingled with it when the meal is sprinkled on cut feed. Feed two or three quarts of the mixture three times daily with a peck of cut hay and straw. If the horse will eat that amount greedily, let the quantity be gradually increased, until he will eat four, five or six quarts at every feeding, three times a day. So long as the animal will eat this allowance, the quantity may be increased a little every day. But always avoid the practice of allowing the horse to stand at a rack well filled with hay. In order to fatten a horse that has run down in flesh, the groom should be very particular to feed the animal no more than he will eat up clean and lick his manger for more. Follow the above suggestions and the result will be satisfactory.

**INTERFERING.** — To prevent interfering in a horse who is turned out in the front feet, the shoe should be applied to fit closely on the inside, and the nails applied round the toe and to the outside. In some instances a small piece of leather placed betwixt the sole and the shoe, and allowed to project outwards, has a very good effect in preventing interfering.

**ITCH.** — To cure a horse affected with itch, first reduce his daily allowance of food, putting him on a low diet, and then give him a teaspoonful of a mixture of equal parts of sulphur and antimony, and at the end of a week or ten days the sores will have disappeared, and the horse will be covered with a fine coat of new hair.

KIDNEYS, INFLAMMATION OF. — (*Nephritis.*) — Symptoms: Gradual loss of flesh, pain accross the back, impaired action of the hind extremities, and the frequent passing of urine, which is very highly colored  In treating this affection, the horse should be allowed perfect rest, and he should also have a generous diet of easily digested food, and plenty of mucilaginous drinks.  The loins may be rubbed every third or fourth day with mustard, and one drachm of tartar emetic given every night. This medicine can be conveniently administered mixed with the food.

KICKING IN STALL. — To prevent your horse from kicking in the stall, fasten a short trace chain, about two feet long, by a strap to each hind foot.  A better way is to have the stalls made wide enough so that the horse can turn in them easily.  Close them with a door or bars, and turn the animal loose.  After a while he will forget the habit, and stand tied without further trouble.

KNEE-PAN DISPLACED. — Feed the horse well on oats, barley, and sound hay; give him a drachm of powdered phosphate of iron daily in his food ; keep in a stall with a perfectly smooth and level floor, and not less than five and a half or six feet wide; apply a shoe with a bar welded to the toe, projecting two or three inches, and then let it be turned up ; rub the joint with an ointment made of one drachm of powdered cantharides to half an ounce of lard, repeating the application next day if it has not blistered.  When a blister rises, wash it off with soap and warm water, and then anoint the part daily with lard, until the scab and other effects have passed off, when another blister may be applied.

KNEE-SPRUNG. — The best remedy for knee-sprung, or contracted tendons, is a winter's run in a straw yard, or a summer's run at grass.

LAMPAS. — This consists in a swelling of the first bar of the upper palate.  It is cured by rubbing the swelling two or three times a day, with one-half an ounce of alum and the same quantity of double refined sugar mixed with a little honey.

**LEGS, INFLAMMATION AND SWELLING OF.** — Rest, and the application of an active blister to the swollen parts, will effect a cure. No better blister can be used than the following: Take resin and black pitch each four parts, beeswax three parts, sweet oil eleven parts, Spanish flies six parts, euphorbium two parts. Melt the resin, pitch and wax first, then add the oil, and when thoroughly mixed remove from the fire; lastly, add very slowly the powdered flies and euphorbium. Before the blister is applied, the hair should be cut close off, and the skin, if scurfy, washed with Castile soap and warm water, after which it must be thoroughly dried, and the blistering ointment rubbed in for ten minutes. After applying the blister, the horse's head should be tied up to prevent his biting the part, or rubbing it with his nose. At the expiration of two or three days most horses may be set at liberty. In about a week rub sweet oil over the blistered part.

**LEGS, BROKEN, TO CURE.** — Instead of summarily shooting the horse, in the greater number of fractures it is only necessary to partially sling the horse by means of a broad piece of sail or other strong cloth, placed under the animal's belly, furnished with two breechings, and two breast-girths, and, by means of ropes and pulleys attached to a cross beam above, he is elevated or lowered, as may be required. By the adoption of this plan, every facility is allowed for the satisfactory treatment of the fractures.

**LINIMENT FOR THE GALLED BACKS OF HORSES.** — White lead moistened with milk. When milk is not to be procured, oil may be substituted. One or two ounces mixed at a time will be sufficient for a month.

**LINIMENT FOR BRUISES, SPRAINS, ETC.** — Take one pint of alcohol, four ounces of Castile soap, one-quarter ounce of gum camphor, one-quarter ounce of sal ammoniac. When these are dissolved, add one ounce of laudanum, one ounce origanum, one half ounce oil of sassafras, and two ounces spirits of hartshorn. Bathe freely.

**LINIMENT, NERVE AND BONE.** — Take beef's gall one quart, alcohol one pint, volatile liniment one pound, spirits of turpentine one pound, oil of origanum four ounces, aqua ammonia four ounces, tincture of Cayenne one-fourth pint, oil of amber three ounces, tincture of Spanish flies six ounces. Mix.

**MOON EYE.** — Moon eye is a term applied to remittent inflammation of the eyes of the horse. From the remittent or periodical appearance of this disease. it has been supposed that it recurred monthly, or with special changes of the moon — hence the name Moon Eye or Moon Blinding. It is constitutional hereditary disease, localizing itself in the eyes. This malady attacks alike the young and the aged, the fat and the lean, while the high bred and the mongrel, the lazy and the nervous, are all equally prone to its baleful influence. Certain kinds of eyes — especially the small sunken eye — seem disposed to contract the disease. Of all the influences tending to the development of moon eye, none is more clearly established than the hereditary predisposition. During its prevalence the animal is almost entirely useless.

Mouth, Sore. — Symptoms: The mouth runs water, the horse cuds, or throws hay out of his mouth. The cause of this disease is often from frosted bits being put into their mouths, or by eating poisoned weeds. To cure, take of borax three drachms, two drachms of sugar of lead, one-half ounce of alum, one pint of vinegar, one pint of sage tea. Shake all well together, and wash the animal's mouth out every morning. Give him no hay for twelve days.

The Mule. — There seems to be but little doubt that mules are more economical than horses for farming purposes. The expense of shoeing mules is much less than that of shoeing horses, on account of the smallness of their feet, the hardness of the hoof, and its freedom from disease.

Mule, Splint on. — To remove these bony formations, the treatment consists in repeated blistering. Having first cut the hair short, rub a little of the following ointment into the skin, covering the splint, every night, until a free watery discharge is produced from the surface: Take of biniodide of mercury two drachms, lard, one ounce. Mix. If after an interval of a fortnight, the splint does not appear much reduced in size, the ointment should be re-applied and repeated at similar intervals.

Nasal Gleet — or running at the nose — can be cured by taking one-half a pound of resin, one-half a pound of blue vitriol, and four ounces of ginger, grinding them all fine, and giving the horse a spoonful two or three times a day.

Navicular Disease. — Symptoms : To prevent tension of the injured parts the horse points his foot. Pointing is also observed in corns and in bruises and injuries of the heel; but long-continued pointing is to be dreaded as the harbinger of incurable lameness. Lameness at first is often slight, and disappears after one-half an hour's work, from increased secretion of syndia. In lifting his foot the horse bends his knee less than natural, and — especially when first brought out — walks on his toe; the toe of the shoe wears rapidly, while the heel exhibits very slight wear. The horse steps or moves in a stilty sort of way. In from four to eight weeks the hoof becomes deeper, narrower at the heels; the sole becomes very concave, and the foot appears no wider at the sole than at the coronet. When the foot, and especially the elastic and insensible frog, ceases to bear weight, it becomes absorbed, the quarters consequently contract, and the sole ascends. This is most on horses used on hard roads and paved streets; rapidity of action is the cause in a great many instances. *Treatment.* — In such cases the practice of paring the quarters almost to the quick is adopted. The toe is shortened, and the feet are enveloped in poultices for ten days, renewing the poultice twice a day. The horse should be fed on bran and oats scalded, with a moderate allowance of hay. Give a dose of opening medicine at the end of ten days; blister the coronet, and keep the hoof moist with wet cloths. The sole may now be thinned, and the horse kept standing on wet sawdust, and a second blister may be at the same time applied. When the horse is shod for work, a leather sole should be applied, and the space between the foot and sole stuffed with tar and tow. Turning the horse into a damp pasture for six weeks will be attended with benefit. In a great many instances this disease is incurable.

OINTMENT, HOOF. — Take one-half a pound of lard and four ounces of rozin. Heat them over a slow fire until melted ; take the pot off the fire, add one ounce of pulverized verdigris ; stir well to prevent it from running over. When partially cool add two ounces of turpentine. Apply it from the hair down one inch. Work the horse all the time.

OINTMENT, SLOAN'S. — Resin four ounces, beeswax four ounces, lard eight ounces, honey two ounces. Melt these articles slowly, gently bringing to a boil ; and, as it begins to boil, remove from the fire and slowly add a little less than a pint of spirits of turpentine, stirring all the time this is being added, and stir until cool.

OVER-REACHING. — Make the shoe its natural length, or a trifle longer — with the calk of the forward shoes high and the heel calk low. The hoof will then stand farther forward, and be more removed from the stride of the hind foot, which, being shod with a low toe calk and high heel calk, will strike the ground before it reaches the fore foot. An interfering horse generally strikes with the inside of the hoof, about two inches from the toe ; therefore make the shoe straighter on the inside, and rasp the hoof accordingly.

PALSY. — An attack of this kind is frequently followed by wasting of the affected muscles — they lose their rounded form, and present a more or less withered aspect. The most common causes of this disease are idleness and plethora. It may result from accidental violence, as blows or falls. *Treatment.* — First, apply a blister over the loins. Then give the mare one of the following pills every morning for eight or ten days : Take gentian and ginger of each two drachms, linseed meal four drachms, strychnine five grains. Mix with water for one pill. The diet should be light, and the mare kept quiet in the stable, or — better — a box stall.

PHYSIC BALL. — Barbadoes aloes four, five or six drachms (according to the size and strength of the horse). tartrate of potassia one drachm, of ginger and Castile soap of each two drachms, anise or peppermint twenty drops ; pulverize. and make all into one ball with thick gum solution. Before giving a horse physic, he should be prepared for it by feeding scalded bran, in place of oats, for two days at the least, giving also water which has the chill taken off, and continue this feed and drink during its operation. If it should not operate in forty-eight hours, repeat one-half the dose.

PNEUMONIA, ACUTE. — *Symptoms.* — They are first taken with a dry, depressed cough, loss of appetite, but thirsty ; pulse feeble, but frequently the extremities are cold — sometimes when first taken, at others they retain their natural heat until the disease assumes its worst appearance, and then the legs become cold. Respiration is very active and laborious ; the animal pants all the time, stands with fore legs widely separated, never lies down, and is loth to move. Some discharge copiously from both nostrils a thick, slimy matter, sometimes mixed with blood — in that case the whole body is excessively hot, and the extremities also, but other symptoms the same. The treatment in the early stage of this disease should be : 1. An abundant supply of cool, fresh air. 2. Abstinence from grain or corn. 3. Extra clothing and warm bandages to the legs. In all cases it is desirable that the patient should at once be removed to an airy, loose box.

POLL EVIL. — If there is only swelling and slight tenderness, but without any fluctuation or pressure from contained matter, give the horse as a laxative five drams of Barbadoes aloes, and rub the poll actively with an ointment made by mixing equal parts of mercurial and iodine ointments. Repeat this application, if necessary, to induce some blistering action. If matter is already formed, as indicated by the fluctuation or pressure, the swelling should be at once opened so as to let it escape. An opening should then be made from the very lowest point of the sac, so that the matter may flow freely as soon as formed. If obstinate, it may be injected several times a week, with a lotion containing one-half a dram of chloride of zinc to a pint of water.

POLL EVIL. (*Norwegian cure.*) — Cover the head and neck with two or three blankets ; have a pan or kettle of the best warm cider vinegar ; then hold it under the blankets ; steam the parts by putting hot stones, brick, or iron into the vinegar, and continue the operation until the horse perspires freely ; do this for three mornings, and skip three, until nine steamings have been accomplished.

POLL EVIL *and* FISTULA. — Common potash one-fourth ounce, extract of belladonna one half drachm, gum Arabic one-fourth ounce. Dissolve the gum in as little water as practicable ; then, having pulverized the potash, unless it is moist, mix the gum water with it and it will soon dissolve ; then mix in the extract and it is ready to use ; it can be used without the belladonna, but is more painful without it and does not have quite as good an effect. The best plan to get this into the pipes is by means of a small syringe, after having cleansed the sore with soap-suds ; repeat once in two days, until all the callous pipes and hard fibrous base around the poll evil or fistula is completely destroyed.

POWDERS, CONDITION. — Two ounces resin, two ounces saltpetre, two ounces black antimony, two ounces sulphur, two ounces saleratus, two ounces ginger, one ounce copperas. One tablespoonful to a dose once a day for three days ; then skip two or three days, and give again until you have given in this way nine doses, or even more if you like. It should be given in the spring and fall, or at any time when the animal is not doing well.

POWDERS, CLEANSING. — Take of ginger two ounces, four ounces fenugreek, one ounce black antimony, and two ounces rhubarb. Grind all fine, mix it well, and it is fit for use. Give a large spoonful every morning and night. It gives a good appetite, and fine coat and life to the animal.

QUITTOR. — The treatment of this disease is as follows : After the shoe has been removed, thin the sole until it will yield to the pressure of the thumb ; then cut the under parts of the wall in an oblique direction from the heel to the anterior part, immediately under the seat of complaint, and only as far as it extends, and rasp the side of the wall thin enough to give way to the pressure of the over-distended parts, and put on a bar-shoe rather elevated from the frog. Ascertain with a probe the direction of the sinuses, and introduce into them a saturated solution of sulphate of zinc, by means of a small syringe. Place over this dressing the common poultice, or the turpentine ointment, and renew the application every twenty-four hours. Three or four such applications will complete a cure. It is recommended that when the probe is introduced, in order to ascertain the progress of the cure, that it be gently and carefully used, otherwise, it may break down the new-formed lymph.

HORSE, HOW TO RIDE A. — The body of the rider is divided into three parts, of which two are movable and one immovable. One of the first consists of all the upper part of the body down to the waist, the other of the lower part of the leg from the knee down. The immovable portion is from the waist to the knees. The rider should sit perfectly square on the middle of the saddle, the upper part of the body presenting a free and unconstrained appearance, the chest not very much thrown forward, the ribs resting freely on the hips, the waist and loins not stiffened, and thus not exposed to tension or efforts from the motions of the horse; the upper part of the body should lean slightly to the rear, rather than forward ; the thighs, inclining a little forward, lie flat and firmly on the saddle, covering the surcingle, of which only a small part behind the knee should be seen ; the lower part of the leg, hanging vertically from the knees, touches the horse, but without the slightest pressure ; the toes are pointed up without constraint, and on the same line with the knees, for if the toes are turned outward, it not only causes the horse to be unnecessarily pricked by the spurs (if worn), but the firmness of the seat is lost ; the heels should be seven-eighths of an inch below the toes; and the stirrups so adjusted that when the rider raises himself on them, there may be the breadth of four fingers between the crotch and the saddle ; to make this adjustment, when the rider has acquired a firm and correct seat, he should, without changing that seat, push the bottom of the stirrup to the hollow of the foot, and then, with the foot horizontal, feel a slight support from the stirrup; when this is accomplished he replaces the foot properly in the stirrup, and the heel will then be seven-eighths of an inch below the toes.

To give the rider a correct seat, the instructor, having caused him to mount, seizes the lower part of his leg, and stretches it straight towards the fore-quarters of the horse, so as to bring the buttocks of the rider square on the saddle; then, resting one hand on the man's knee, he seizes the lower part of the leg with the other, and carries back the thigh and knee so as to bring the crotch square on the saddle, the thighs covering the surcingle, the lower part of the leg, from the knee down, also over the surcingle, and sees that the rider does not sit too much on his crotch, but has his buttocks well under him. He then explains to the rider that the firmness of the seat consists in this: that the rider grasps the horse with his legs; that both thighs press equally upon the saddle, in conformity with the movements of the body, and that the general movements of the body and thighs must conform to those of the horse. He should be taught, too, how to hold the feet, without allowing him to place them in the stirrups, for this is one of the most essential conditions for a good seat.

RINGBONE. — This disease is generally caused by heavy draught, especially in up-hill work. The first appearance of the complaint is indicated by a hard swelling upon the top of the fetlock or pastern joint, accompanied by tenderness, pain, heat, etc. Cooling appliances, such as cold water, soap, camphor, etc., with a little laudanum, should be promptly applied, giving the animal perfect rest, with green food or roots in connection with hay — no grain. This may be followed by some convenient preparation of iodine, like an ointment of iodide of lead and lard. Rub in the ointment well, and follow up the treatment for several weeks. If the case is an obstinate one, try blistering with cerate of cantharides, continuing, at intervals, the use of the iodine. Equal parts of turpentine and kerosene would no doubt form a most excellent wash — the crude coal oil would be better than that which has been refined. Rub it well into the hair around and above the hoof.

RINGBONE REMEDIES. — Pulverized cantharides, oils of spike, origanum, amber, cedar, Barbadoes tar, and British oil, of each two ounces; oil of wormwood one ounce, spirits of turpentine four ounces, common potash one-half ounce, nitric acid six ounces, oil of vitriol (sulphuric acid) four ounces, and lard three pounds. Melt the lard and slowly add the acids; stir well and add the others, stirring until cold. Clip off the hair, and apply by rubbing and heating in; in about three days, or when it is done running, wash off with suds and apply again. In old cases it may take three or four weeks, but in recent cases two or three applications will cure. — 2. Take one-half pint spirits of turpentine, one-half ounce blue stone, one-half ounce of red precipitate. Shake well and use every morning; and keep the hoof well greased. This will not only take off the hair, but cause a severe blister. After healing, if there still be signs of lameness, repeat the remedy.

RINGWORM. — Wash the parts with a very strong infusion of bayberry bark, wipe dry, and then smear the denuded spots with a mixture of four ounces of pyroligneous acid, one ounce of turpentine, the washing and dressing to be repeated until healthy action is established. If the disease does not readily disappear, give sulphur, cream of tartar, and sassafras, equal parts, in a dose of six drachms daily. If the disease still lingers, sponge the denuded parts with tincture of muriate iron.

RUNAWAY HORSES, To prevent injuries from. — This can be done by electricity. A complete electric apparatus can be purchased in a small case. Let one of these be fixed in an out-of-the-way nook in the carriage, two wires to hook to harness, beneath which have two very thin copper plates properly placed. In the event of a runaway, the driver and inside occupants will only have to press a glass knob to stop instantly the mad career of the strongest horses.

RUPTURE. — Rupture or hernia is the protrusion of a bowel, or some other part, from its proper cavity. It is sometimes congenital, and may then be produced at the same time that castration is performed. At other times rupture may be produced by blows, kicks, or falls. A hernia is dangerous to life when it becomes compressed or strangulated by a stricture at the orifice of protrusion. Skilful surgical aid should always be obtained in any such case at once. But sometimes, in the absence of a veterinarian, any one may restore the gut by introducing the hand into the bowel and drawing it up; the other hand, at the same time, making gentle pressure upon the swelling in the abdomen. No violence should ever be used in attempting this; and the bowels should first be emptied by a clyster.

SCRATCHES. — If a horse's blood is pure he will not have the scratches. Give him a tablespoonful of saltpetre every day for fifteen days, and be careful about his taking cold while feeding it. It opens the pores so that he will take cold very easy. Along with this take pure, dry white lead, pure oxide of zinc and glycerine, of each half an ounce; fresh lard (free from rancidity) one and one half-ounce. Mix the white lead, oxide of zinc, and glycerine, to a uniform, smooth paste, then add the lard, a little at a time, till a uniform, smooth ointment is formed. Wash the parts with Castile soap and water, and dry with a cloth, then apply the ointment two or three times daily with the fingers. Wash once in two or three days, and dry the spot well before dressing again.

The horse should stand on a plank floor kept clean and dry; and if used, all dust, sand and dirt should be washed off so that the affected parts may remain clean. If these directions are strictly carried out, it will seldom, if ever, fail to cure the very worst cases within a reasonable time.

Shoeing Horses. — Few horseshoers understand thoroughly the anatomy of the horse's foot. The great mistake is made in attempting to trim the hoof to fit the shoe, whereas the shoe should be made to fit the hoof. Very little trimming is needed if the shoe is made right. The frog should never be touched by the buttress, if the foot is healthy, as Nature has intended that to be the spring or cushion to first receive the blow when the foot is set down on the road, to guard the knee and shoulder from the concussion.

Nothing can be more barbarous than the carving and cutting of a horse's foot before shoeing, though on his skill in this many a farrier prides himself. The idea that the frog must not be allowed to bear on the ground — that the sole must be thinned till it " springs on the thumb," is a most pernicious one.

As you value your horse, do not let the blacksmith even scrape the dirt off the frog. It would be better if he could not see it, because, if anything fit to be called a frog, he will beg, argue, and try every means to persuade you to let him cut it. Do not turn your back to him while he has the foot in his lap and knife in his hand, or else off comes a portion of the frog. If the frog is left to itself, it will, when nature gets ready, shed itself; but the difference between shedding and cutting is, that before shedding the under frog is protected by a suitable covering, but when cut it is exposed to the action of the air and water, which causes it to crack, leaving those " rags " which the blacksmith loves so well to cut. Do not open the heels, as it increases the resistance offered to contraction.

The summer shoe needs to present a flat surface to the ground. Make it of the same width and thickness from the toe to the heel. Have the seating deep, so as to prevent the sole pressing upon the shoe as it descends. Have a clip at the toe to prevent the shoe slipping back, but none at the sides, as they not only destroy too much of the hoof, but prevent expansion. Have the fullering deep to receive the nail-heads, and have the nail holes straight — neither inclined inwardly or outwardly. Have only five nails to hold on the shoe — two on the inner, and three on the outside. Place the two on the inner side about one and a half inches from the top ; those on the outside may be placed farther back towards the heel. The reason is, that when the foot strikes the ground it expands to relieve the horse of the shock of his weight, and the inner side being thinner than the outside, the expansion is greater. By placing the nails far back we prevent that expansion, thereby cramping the foot, which makes the animal step short and quick, like one with tight boots. If we take an old shoe, we find at the heels that it is worn down, and also that it is smaller and bright, which is not done by the shifting of the shoe, as you only find it at the heels, by the action of the foot while expanding and contracting. Of course, this action wears upon, but the foot is continually growing.

On fitting the shoe, do not let it burn the foot, as it makes a strong foot brittle, and on a weak one hurting the horse. Be sure it fits close to the foot. Bring in the heels, as not they, but the nails prevent expansion. Do not get the nails larger than necessary; bring them out low down in the crust, and make the clinchers very broad. Rasp below but not above the clinchers, as the foot above is covered — if healthy — with a varnish which excludes the air and water.

The hind shoe need not be so broad, but a little higher at the heels. In this put seven nails, as the hind legs propel and the front legs receive the weight.

The winter shoe needs toe and heel pieces to prevent the horse from slipping. Have the inner cork not quite so sharp as the outer one, so that if he steps upon the other foot it will not cut it.

The outside of the hoof ought not to be at all touched by the rasp, save at the very edge, as rasping tends to thicken the hoof and make it coarse and clumsy. Shoes should be made just as light as they possibly can be to answer the purpose. Ordinarily they are one-third too heavy. A horse's hoof should be carefully cleaned every day, and oiling the hoof once or twice a week is recommended.

SPAVIN. — Take one-half ounce oil of amber, one ounce oil of spike, two ounces spirits of turpentine, one-half ounce nitric acid. The acid must be put into the bottle last. Apply this mixture thoroughly, and — though it will not remove the bunch — the lameness will generally disappear. If the horse is over four years old, you will fit a bar of lead just above it, wiring the ends together so that it will constantly wear upon the enlargement, and the two together will cure nine cases out of every ten in six weeks.

SPAVIN CURE. — Take one ounce of origanum oil, one ounce of British oil, one ounce of oil of spike, one ounce oil of wormwood, one ounce gum myrrh, one gill of alcohol. Put the oils together; put the gum in the alcohol, and let it stand for twenty-four hours, and then add it to the oils; shake well before using; apply it to the parts affected, and rub it in well with the hand, or heat it in with a hot iron. If it is applied for a sprain, use it morning and evening. Wash clean once in three days.

SPLINT.—When a splint does not occasion lameness it need not be interfered with. To cure, take volatile liniment (of the U. S. Dispensatory) to which add one dram of oil of origanum. Apply this thoroughly twice a day, followed by rubbing the splint with a round pine or bass wood stick, as hard as can be done without abrading the skin. This treatment should be continued several weeks, when it will be discovered that the splints will grow less and finally disappear.

SPRAINS, GENERAL TREATMENT OF.—Rest is the first requirement. Next apply wet bandages until the heat is abated, and until there is no pain on pressure; then rub with some simple ointment.

STAGGERS.—This is a functional disorder of the brain, which, when once it has declared itself, is said to be beyond cure. The following prescription may be tried. Give a mess twice per week composed of one gal. of bran, one table-spoonful of sulphur, one spoonful of saltpetre, one quart of boiling sassafras tea, one and one-fourth ounces assafetida. Keep the horse from cold water for one-half a day afterwards.

STRANGLES.—Feed with light, cooling (green if it can be had) food; mix the food with sassafras tea, in which a spoonful of powdered sulphur and a teaspoonful of saltpetre have been added.

STIFLE–STEPPING, TO CURE.—One-half a tea-cup of vinegar, the whites of two eggs, a piece of alum the size of a chestnut, well beaten, dissolved and warmed. Twitch and knee-strap the fore leg standing off from the affected member. Apply with the hand and rub it in well; saturate a piece of flannel six inches square, place it over the joint, cover this with a double thickness of the same, long enough to lap behind the leg, and draw it very tight. Now take a very hot flat-iron and iron it, being cautious not to blister your horse too severely. Turn him out, and in one week repeat; in the mean time bathe the parts with a decoction of white-oak bark.

SWEENY.—A horse is said to be sweenied when the muscles of the shoulder appear to have perished away, and the skin seems to be attached closely to the shoulder-blade. These symptoms may arise from chronic lameness in the foot or other part of the limb. In such case, of course it is of no use to apply remedies to the shoulder. Cure the foot, and the shoulder will come right, although stimulants and rubbing will expedite it. But genuine sweeny is quite different from the above, although the appearances are the same. It is caused by hard drawing in a collar that is too large ; or where no whiffletree is ever used, but the traces are hitched directly to the thills, as in "jumpers," as they are called ; or by jumping fences, or the like. The presence of real sweeny may be discovered by moving the horse in a circle, or causing him to step over bars, when you can generally determine the seat of the lameness. For such cases irritants with friction, is the proper treatment. Blistering liniment, or seton, or a piece of leather inserted under the skin, will cure with rest.

TAMING AND TRAINING. — Many persons pay for instructions in training horses, and yet they nearly all fail, simply because, with all the instructions in the world, they cannot handle a horse — it is not in them. To be a successful trainer you must have a sympathy with the horse and a personal power of control. That which partakes of the power necessary to subdue and train, you will find in your own mind, your own love, will and wisdom. If you have little or no instinctive love for the horse, of course you are not the person to control him. Men and women are often found who are said to have the natural gift of controlling the horse; they love horses from instinct, as it were. The secret in these cases consists in their intense love for the horse. If you love the horse, you will, you can but know how to make the horse love you. Love, in all grades of animals, has its appropriate language; and when this language is addressed to the horse, it excites love, of course. A blow with a whip or club does not come from love, but from combativeness, and it excites combativeness or fear in the horse. If you want to make a horse love you (and you must cause him to love you if you control him), why of course you must love him and treat him accordingly. Study the character of your horse — not the nature of horses in general, but of the horse that you wish to control. Horses differ in their dispositions as really as men do, and each one is to be approached, attracted, pleased and controlled accordingly. *To make him Lie Down.* — First, catch your horse, then strap the near fore leg up round the arm of the animal; lead him about on three legs until he becomes tired or weary; he will then allow you to handle him anywhere; then attach a strap with a ring to the off fore-fetlock; to this ring fasten another strap, which being brought over the horse's back to the near side, is put through the ring on the off fore-fetlock; return the end of the strap to the near side, still keeping fast hold, and move the animal on, and pull; he will then be thrown upon his knees, when, after struggling for some time, by gentle usage he will lie down. After unloosing the straps, put him through the same process as before, when the horse will lie down whenever required. Uniformity is necessary in our method. It is by the repetition, by the constant recurrence of certain motions, words, or actions, that we succeed. Many fail for the want of uniformity in their method. They are loving and kind by spells, then they are harsh and cruel. The horse is "impressed," as it is said, with his master's wishes, when those wishes are often and uniformly expressed in motions, words, and actions! If man needs "precept upon precept, line upon line," etc., in order to learn his lessons well, how much more true is this of the horse, which is below man in consciousness and the reflective faculties. *Teaching him to Pace.* — Buckle a four pound weight around the ankles of his hind legs (lead is preferable); ride your horse briskly with these weights upon his ankles, at the same time twitching each rein of the bridle alternately; by this means you will immediately throw him into a pace. After you have trained him in this way to some extent, change your leaded weights for something lighter; leather padding, or something equal to it, will answer the purpose; let him wear these light weights until he is perfectly trained. This process will make a smooth and easy pacer of any horse. *To make him Trot.* — The secret consists in using rollers on the front feet. These rollers are made of pieces of wood or horn turned round, as big as a hickory nut, with a gimlet hole bored through the centre of each, and about twelve of them strung on a string or narrow strap (which should be much smaller than the hole), and then tied or buckled very loose around the feter-lock joint next to the hoof, so that they will play loose up and down when the horse is in motion. As soon as the horse finds something on his feet, he will lift them up higher and throw them out farther and handsomer; this he will soon learn permanently. Another secret is that a small or medium sized flat is the best, and far superior to the track system for teaching the horse or colt to gather quickly. A very light skeleton or gig should be used in training. *To Sit on his Haunches.* — First teach the horse to obey you, so that when you say, "Ho!" he will remain still. Then, having taught him to lie down, let him get up on his fore legs, and then stop him. The horse gets up in this way, and you have only to teach him to hold his position for a while. It does not strain the horse to sit; and you must always use the word "Sit," in connection with the feat; also the word "Down," when you wish him to fall. *To make him Follow you.* — Take your horse to the stable, put on a surcingle and a bridle with short reins, which may be checked up a little and fastened to the surcingle. Then lead him about a few times, and letting go the bridle, continue to caress him, as you constantly say, "Come along." If he lag, give him a light cut behind with a long whip.  Continue this until you succeed.  Do not forget the element of " love " in this as well as other feats.  *To Teach him to Pick up a Handkerchief.* — Spread on the sawdust a white cloth containing a liberal supply of oats; lead the animal round the ring, and let him take some of the oats.  This is lesson No. 1: its object being to fix in the horse's mind a connection between the cloth and the oats.  The march round the circle being once or twice repeated, he stops at the handkerchief as a matter of course.  By dint of practice — say a couple of weeks — he will learn to stop as readily in a trot or a gallop as in a walk.  After a time the handkerchief must be doubled over and tied in a knot; the animal shakes it to get at the grain; but not succeeding, lifts it from the ground, which is just the thing wanted.  When the horse has done this a few times, and finds that, though he can shake nothing out, he will receive a handful of oats as a reward, he may be trusted to perform in public.  The last step of all — persuading the horse to carry the handkerchief to his owner — is easily done.  Of his own accord he will hold the cloth till it is taken from his mouth, and there will be little difficulty in coaxing him to walk a few steps — when he knows that he will get a handful of oats or a carrot for his obedience.  *Teaching him to Walk.* — For every-day use, the most economical gait for a horse is a fast walk; and yet not half the thought is given to this essential that there is to other things that secure to the horse a name rather than intrinsic value.  Colts can be taught to walk fast by following them for a half day together (some one leading) with a small switch, starting them, when inclined to go slow, into a quicker pace.  After they are harnessed, keep fast walking in mind; and when on level ground, or going up a hill with a very light load, urge them to their utmost, until four miles an hour becomes a habit.  *Teaching him to Stand.* — Take your horse on the barn floor, and throw a strap over his back and fasten it to his right fore foot; lead him along, and, " Whoa," and at the same time pull down the strap, which will throw him on three feet, and make him stop suddenly.  This is the best way known to teach " Whoa," though you can put on the war bridle, and give him a sharp jerk that will stop him about as soon as the strap to his foot.  Then put him in harness, with the foot strap, as directed under the head of " Training to Harness," and drive him up to the door.  The moment he undertakes to move, take his foot and say " Whoa."  Get in your carriage and get out again; rattle the thills; make all the noise getting in and out you can; give him to understand, by snatching his foot each time he moves, that he must stand until you tell him to go; and after a few times you can put the whole family in the carriage, and he will not stir out of his tracks.

TAMING, PREPARATION FOR.—Take finely grated horse castor, and oils of rhodium and cummin ; keep these in separate bottles, well corked ; put some of the oil of cummin on your hand, and approach the horse on the windy side. He will then move towards you ; then rub some of the cummin on his nose ; give him a little of the castor on anything he likes, and get eight or ten drops of the oil of rhodium on the point of his tongue ; you can then get him to do anything you please. Follow up your advantage by all the kindness and attention possible towards the animal, and your control is certain.

TENDONS, CONTRACTED. — First try the effect of lowering the heels a little more than the toe at each shoeing, and applying a shoe with a plate projecting an inch or two in front of the toe. If there is much tenderness of the back sinews on pressure, this form of shoeing must be avoided until that has been removed. The thickened tendons must be rubbed daily with a mixture in equal parts of strong iodine ointment and blue ointment, until blistering takes place, when it may be discontinued until the effects have passed off. The horse should have a yard to run in where he is not very likely to be excited to vigorous or irregular action, or, if kept in-doors, let it be in a roomy box, and give a moderate amount of walking exercise daily. Should several months of this sort of treatment fail to restore in part, it may be advisable, perhaps, to have the back sinews cut through.

THRUSH. — This is a discharge of very offensive matter from the cleft of the frog. It is inflammation of the lower surface of the sensible frog, and during which pus is secreted together with or instead of horn. In its treatment, almost any astringent substance will check thrush in its early stage. Tar and common salt mixed is a very good application, and tar and sulphate of zinc can also be highly recommended. Before the introduction of either of these preparations, the frog should be carefully inspected and all decayed parts removed. The dressing must be pressed to the bottom of the cleft and commissures of the frog, and this should be repeated every other day or twice a week.

TRICKS OF HORSE-DEALERS. — Unless a man is accustomed to horses, it is the greatest folly in the world to depend upon his own knowledge in purchasing them, for there is a class of men who make their living by bringing up horses with all manner of defects, and which their art enables them to disguise just as long as is sufficient to take in their dupes. In buying as well as selling are these deceptions practised. A few of these " tricks " are as follows. *To make a True-pulling Horse Baulk.* — Take tincture of cantharides one ounce, and corrosive sublimate one drachm. Mix, and bathe his shoulders freely at night. *To make a Horse appear as if Lame.* — Take a single hair from the tail ; put through the eye of a needle ; lift the front leg, and press the skin between the outer and middle tendon or cord ; shove the needle through ; cut off the hair on each side, and let the foot down ; the horse will go lame in twenty minutes. *To make a Horse stand by his Food and not Eat it.* — Grease the front teeth and the roof of the mouth with common beef tallow, and he will not eat until you have washed it out. *To make a Horse appear as if Badly Foundered.* — Take a fine wire and fasten it around the fetlock, between the foot and heel, and smooth the hair over it. In twenty minutes the horse will show lameness. Do not leave it on over nine hours. *To Cure a Horse of the Crib or Sucking Wind.* — Saw between the upper teeth to the gums. *To Cover up the Heaves.* — Drench the horse with one-fourth pound of common bird shot, and he will not heave until they pass through him. *To make a Horse appear as if he had the Glanders.* — Melt four ounces of fresh butter and pour it into his ear. *To Nerve a Horse that is Lame.* — Make a small incision about half way from the knee to the joint on the outside of the leg, and at the back part of the shin bone you will find a small white tendon or cord ; cut it off and close the external wound with a stitch, and he will walk off on the hardest pavement and not limp a particle. *To Disguise Lameness.* — When a horse goes dead lame in one shoulder, it can be disguised by creating a similar lameness in the corresponding leg, by taking off the shoe and inserting a bean between it and the foot. *To put Black Spots on a White Horse.* — Take of powdered quicklime one-half a pound, and litharge four ounces. Well beat and mix the litharge with the lime. The above is to be put into a vessel, and a sharp ley is to be poured over it. Boil and skim off the substance which rises on the surface. This is the coloring matter, which must be applied to such parts of the animal as you wish to have dyed black. *To Produce a Star on a Horse.* — Take a piece of tow-linen, the size of the wished-for star ; spread on it warm pitch, and apply it to the shaved spot ; leave it on for two or three days, when wash with a little asmart water, or elixir of vitriol, two or three times a day until well. When the hair grows it will be white. *To make an Old Horse appear Young.* — This is done by filing down the teeth, the dark markings on which are removed by a hot iron. Filling up the depressions over the horse's eyes, by puncturing the skin over the cavity, and filling through a tube by air from the mouth, and then closing the aperture, when the brow will become smooth — for a time. The white hairs are painted out, when the animal will altogether have a youthful appearance.

URINE, STOPPAGE OF — Symptoms: Frequent attempts to urinate, looking round at his sides, lying down, rolling and stretching. To cure, take one-half pound of hops, three drachms oil of camphor; grind and mix. Make this into three pills. Give one every day, with a drench made of a small spoonful of saltpetre and two ounces of water. This will cure, as a general thing.

WARTS, TO CURE. — The safest and most effectual caustic for destroying warts is chromic acid. Having first picked off the rough outer surface of the warts so as to make them bleed, apply, by means of a small wooden spatula, a little of the dry acid, rubbing it well in. This will cause a free discharge of watery fluid from the surface. In a few days the wart is converted into a tough, leather-like substance, which ultimately falls off, generally leaving a healthy sore, which soon heals.

WARTS ON A HORSE'S NOSE. — Dissolve one-half pound of alum in a quart of water; with a brush or cloth wet the warts twice each day for four days, and they will disappear.

WATER FARCIN. — Symptoms: The horse is dull and loses his appetite, and swells along the belly or chest and between the fore legs. To cure: Rowel in the breast, and along each side of the chest, as far as the swelling goes. Leave the rowels in until the swelling goes down; give a spoonful of cleansing powders morning and night.

WEN, TO CURE A. — Take equal parts of soft soap and slaked lime, well mixed. Lance the wen at the time of making the application, or two or three days after. Two or three applications will cure.

WIND-GALLS. — Wind-galls are puffy swellings above and behind the fetlocks, caused by the enlargement of the sheaths through which the tendons pass. In recent cases nothing further is required than rest, aperient medicine, and wet bandages wrapped firmly around the swellings. It may also be advisable to remove the shoe and shorten the toe to remove the tension of the tendons. When there is lameness, and the swelling is indurated, hot fomentations for several hours a day, or poultices, should be applied. A woolen bandage should afterwards be applied, and camphorated spirits well rubbed in daily.

WIND IN HORSES, TO IMPROVE. — It will be found, if tar water and powdered charcoal are mixed with the horse's feed, that it will have a most beneficial effect on his wind and condition.

Worms in Horses. — 1. Give every morning, one hour before feeding, three drachms of sulphate of iron and two drachms of assafœtida; and every night, for a week, throw up an injection of one ounce oil of turpentine and ten ounces of linseed oil. Green food is to be preferred. 2. White-ash bark burnt to ashes and made into rather a very strong ley; then mix half a pint of it with one pint of warm water, and give it all two or three times daily.

Breasts, Sore. — A thorough application of strong alum water or white oak bark to the breast of the animal, three days before going to work, will toughen them so that they will not get sore. Another excellent plan is, when you let your team rest for a few moments during work, to raise the collar and pull it a little forward, and rub the breast thoroughly with your naked hand.

Breaking Down. — The suspensory ligament is attached superiorly to the back of the knee, and inferiorly to the back of the fetlock joint. It is elastic and gives springiness to the limb. In motion and in standing it passively supports the horse's fetlock. If this ligament is torn or cut across, the joint comes to the ground and the toe turns up; if severely strained, the fetlock descends unnaturally low. In breaking down, the fetlock is almost completely torn across, and the fetlocks come nearly or completely to the ground. Considerable swelling soon ensues above and behind the fetlock; there is great pain and symptomatic fever, and in severe cases the tendons are generally sprained. When the suspensory ligament is completely ruptured, and where the injury occurs in both fore legs, treatment need not be attempted. In severe cases the leg should be immersed in a pail of water, and kept in it for several days. When the pain and fever subside, wet bandages may be used. A dose of opening medicine should also be given. Bran mashes and hay should constitute the horse's diet at the first, and when pain and fever subside the diet may be more liberal. In bad cases a high-heeled shoe may be applied, or the horse may be slung so as to relieve the affected leg of weight.

Blood, Fulness of. — When this condition appears, the eyes appear heavy, dull, red or inflamed, and are frequently closed as if asleep; the pulse is small and oppressed; the heat of the body somewhat increased; the legs swell; the hair also rubs off. Horses that are removed from grass to a warm stable, and full fed on hay and corn, and not sufficiently exercised, are very subject to one or more of these symptoms. By regulating the quantity of food given to him, by proper exercise and occasional laxatives, a cure may soon be effected.

3*

BOWELS, LOOSE.— In cases of chronic diarrhœa, a good remedy is to put powdered charcoal in the feed, and if the disease depends on a digestive function — the liver included — give a few doses of the following: Powdered golden seal two ounces, ginger one ounce, salt one ounce. Dose one-half an ounce twice a day.

BOTS.— Bots are the larvæ of the gad fly, of which there are three different kinds. The female gad fly, during the summer months, deposits her ova on the horses' legs or sides, and they become firmly attached to the hair. After remaining on the leg for some time, perhaps four or five days, they become ripe, and at this time the slightest application of warmth and moisture is sufficient to bring forth the latent larvæ. At this period, if the tongue of the horse chances to touch the egg, its operculum is thrown open, and a small worm is produced, which readily adheres to the tongue, and with the food is conveyed into the stomach, and therein is lodged and hatched. It clings to the cuticular coat by means of its tenacula, between which is its mouth; and in such a firm manner does it adhere to the lining of the stomach, that it will suffer its body to be pulled asunder without quitting its hold. Bots are often supposed to do a good deal of harm, but except in cases where they accumulate in very large numbers, we are of the opinion that they are almost harmless, because in ordinary cases they are chiefly attached to the cuticular coat, and the cuticular coat of the stomach is not possessed of a great degree of sensibility. Most horses that have been running at pasture during the summer months become affected more or less with bots, and their presence in the stomach is thus accounted for. When a horse is troubled with the bots, it may be known by the occasional nipping at their own sides, and by red pimples and projections on the inner surface of the upper lip, which may be seen plainly by turning up the lip. To remove them, take of new milk two quarts, molasses one quart, and give the horse the whole amount. Fifteen minutes afterward give two quarts of very warm sage tea, and thirty minutes after the tea give one pint of linseed oil (or enough to operate as a physic). Lard has been used, when the oil could not be obtained, with the same success. The cure will be complete, as the milk and molasses cause the bots to let go their hold, the tea puckers them up, and the oil carries them entirely away. The spring is the only season in which there is a chance to effectually remove them.

CATARACT.— This can be removed from a horse's eye with finely pulverized burnt alum, blown into the horse's eye through a goose quill. Or take oil of wintergreen, get a small glass syringe, and inject a few drops into the eye, and after three days repeat the application.

CATARRH, NASAL, OR CORYZA.— This malady is commonly known as a cold; it is an inflammation of the membrane lining the interior of the nose, and is observed in all the domestic animals. It occurs frequently after sudden changes in the temperature of the atmosphere, which checks or diminishes largely the action of the skin. In the early stage the animal is feverish; the membrane of the nose is dry and infected; the animal also frequently sneezes and coughs. There is a watery mucus discharge from one or both nostrils, which by degrees assumes a yellowish color. In young animals this affection is generally associated with swellings beneath the jaws. When the disease extends over a longer period than a fortnight it assumes a chronic type. *Treatment.*— Dissolve one-half an ounce of nitre in a pint of water, and administer this to the patient daily, or it may be mixed with the water which the horse drinks. A bran mush should be given every other day. When the disease assumes a chronic form, which is seldom the case, injecting the nose with a weak solution of alum will remove the discharge. Young horses are very apt to have swelled legs unless they get walking exercise for a short time every day. This is owing partly to the weakness of the circulation, and partly to a deteriorated state of the blood having been engendered during the horse's sickness.

CASTRATION.— A most important point to be considered is the proper time for the operation to be performed, and when that is satisfactorily decided, employ none other than a thoroughly competent individual to assume the duty. Very many of the defects observable in geldings are attributable to too early or too late a period of castration, and might have been, in a great measure, avoided by a judicious selection of the time suitable for its occurrence. A colt whose development will warrant his being cut at five or six months of age, will be in very slight danger from the operation; but few are so formed, much the larger number requiring a year's full growth to sufficiently perfect them, and others exceeding even that age. The withers, neck and shoulders are the most frequently deficient, and are parts that are most dependent upon castration for their proper appearance in the horse. The weather of late spring or early autumn will be found the most suitable time for castrating, when the air is dry and temperate. Upon no consideration should the animal, after being cut, be exposed to wet or inclement weather, or unsheltered from too hot a sun. Close confinement, or unlimited exercise, is equally prejudicial to an early and successful healing of the parts, and moderate liberty should in all cases be allowed the patient.

Speaking of the operation, Mr. Youatt says: "The old method of opening the scrotum (testicle bag) on either side, and cutting off the testicles, and preventing bleeding by a temporary compression of the vessels, while they are being seared with a hot iron, must not, perhaps, be abandoned; but there is no necessity of that extra pain, when the spermatic cord (the blood vessels and the nerve) is compressed between two pieces of wood as tightly as in a vise, and then left until the following day, or until the testicle drops off." He also objects to the unnecessary pain inflicted upon colts by corping them, and states that it is accompanied with considerable danger. With regard to the method of castration by Torison, he adds: "An incision is made into the scrotum, and the *vas deferens* is exposed and divided; the artery is then seized by a pair of forceps contrived for the purpose, and is then twisted round six or seven times. It retracts without untwisting the coils, and bleeding ceases, the testicle is removed, and there is no sloughing or danger. The most painful part of the operation, which is that of the firing-irons or the clamps is avoided, and the wound readily heals."

CLICKING.— This is noticeable by a disagreeable clicking noise made by the horse striking the toe of his hind shoe against the inner edge of the fore one. To prevent this annoying habit, shoe the hind foot short at the toe — that is to say, set the shoe as far back as is compatible with security and safety; the fore shoe should be forged narrow with the inner margin filed round and smooth.

COLIC, SYMPTOMS:  The horse often lies down, and suddenly rises again with a spring; strikes his belly with his hind feet, stamps with his fore feet, and refuses every kind of food, etc. The following is said never to fail in curing cases of colic: Aromatic spirits of ammonia one-half an ounce, laudanum one and a half ounce; mix with one pint of water, and administer. If not relieved, repeat the dose in a short time. Another and a better remedy is to take a piece of carpet, blanket, or any thick material, large 'enough to cover the horse from his fore to his hind legs, and from the spine to the floor as he lies, and wring it out in hot water as hot as you can stand. You need not fear scalding the animal. Apply this to the horse, and cover it with a similar dry cloth. As soon as the heat diminishes much, dip the wet cloth again in hot water.

COLLAR, HOW TO FIT A HORSE. — An excellent plan, and one that will not injure the collar, is to dip it in water until the leather is thoroughly wet, then put it on the horse, secure the hames firmly, keeping it there until it becomes dry. It is all the better if heavy loads are to be drawn, as that causes the collar to be more evenly fitted to the neck and shoulder. If possible, the collar should be kept on from four to five hours, when it will be perfectly dry, and retain the same shape ever afterwards; and as it is exactly fitted to the form of the neck, will not produce chafes, nor sores on the horse's neck.

CORNS. — Corns occur to horses with the best of feet. The high heeled and contracted quartered, the low as well as the broad, all occasionally become afflicted with this annoying disease, the common cause being the worst of shoeing. Success in the treatment of corns must rest entirely upon the intelligent understanding of the shoer. If he is master of the art, he will see at a glance what parts of the foot require to be removed. In the preparation of the foot no matter what its form, so long as there is no reason to suspect suppuration, no " paring out the corn " should be permitted. When such officious exploration is permitted, the healthy condition of the whole foot is interfered with; the scooping out of the horn, at the angle formed by the wall and bar interferes with the natural growth of these parts, causes them to tilt over and to press directly upon the seat of the corn, thus inflicting injuries which frequently terminate in suppuration. Let the horse's foot be properly adjusted in all its parts, always leaving as broad and level a bearing surface as possible. With regard to the shoe, unless the condition of the horse's foot requires some special modification for its protection, we prefer a plain shoe, a small clip at the toe, moderately broad web, and of uniform thickness from toe to heel.

COLTS, THEIR CARE AND MANAGEMENT. — Much harm arises from improper weaning. A good method is, when the colt is four or five months old, to put a strong halter upon him, place him in a stall, and put his mother in an adjoining stall, with a partition between, so arranged that they can see each other, and, if possible, get their heads together. The first day let the colt nurse twice — the next day once. Feed the mare upon dry hay and dry feed, and about half milk her two or three times a day until dry. · Feed the colt upon new-mown grass or fine clover hay, and give him a pint of oats twice per day, and in about two weeks you will have your colt weaned, and your mare dry, and your colt looking as well as ever. When he is one year old he has as much growth and development of muscle as one two years old weaned in the usual manner. When the mare becomes dry, colt and mare may be again turned in pasture. An opinion generally prevails among farmers that, from the time the foal is taken from its dam up to coming to maturity, it should not be "pushed," as the saying is, nor fed on grain, for fear it would injure one so young and tender. This accounts for the great number of moping or spiritless and unthrifty colts that are scarcely able to drag one leg after another. Their very appearance, cadaverous and pitiful looks, seem to convey to the mind of every sensible man that they are the victims of a wretched system of starvation, which enervates the digestive organs, impairs the secretions, and impoverishes the blood. Hence the deficiency in the development of bone and muscle. The muscles and tendons, being so illy supplied with material for growth and development, become very weak, and afford but little support to the bones and joints, so that the former become crooked and the latter weak — defects which no after feeding, no skill in training can counteract. It must be known to breeders that from the time of birth up to maturity, colts require food abounding in flesh-making principle, nitrogenous compounds — oats, corn, etc.; otherwise they must naturally be deficient in size, symmetry, and powers of endurance. Therefore they should be regularly fed and watered ; and their food should consist of ground oats, wheat bran, and sweet hay, in quantities sufficient to promote their growth. Finally, proper shelter should always be provided for them. They should not be exposed, as they often are, to the vicissitudes of the weather, under the false notion of making them tough and hardy. Equally unwise is it to confine colts to close, unventilated, and filthy stables, deprived of light, exercise, and pure air. They should be groomed every day; a clean skin favors the vitalization of the blood. They should be permitted to gambol about as much as they choose. Exercise develops muscle, makes an animal active and spirited, and increases the capacity of the lungs and chest. By the above means, and proper attention to the principles of breeding, the business of raising colts may become both creditable and profitable.

COLT, TO PREVENT FROM JUMPING. — Pass a good stout surcingle around his body; put on his halter, and have the halter strap long enough to go from his head, between his fore legs, then through the surcingle, and back to one of his hind legs. Procure a thill strap, and buckle around the leg between the foot and joint; fasten the halter strap in this — shorter or longer, as the obstinacy of the case may require. It is also useful to keep colts from running where there is likely to be danger from the result. If the thill strap should cause any soreness on the leg, it may be wound with a woolen cloth, and it would be well to change from one leg to the other occasionally.

COLT, CALLUS ON. — Take one ounce of bitter sweet, one ounce of skunk cabbage, one ounce of blood root ; steep and mix with lard ; make an ointment, and apply once or twice a day. This is considered a sure remedy.

COUGH. — Take powdered squills one ounce, ginger two ounces, cream of tartar one ounce ; mix well, and give a spoonful every morning in bran. Another remedy is to give the animal a feed of sunflower seed.

CRIBBING. — There is supposed to be no remedy for this habit, but a person who has tried it says that a horse can be cured of cribbing by nailing a sheepskin, wool side up, wherever there is any chance for the horse to bite.

DISTEMPER. — The treatment of distemper should consist in good nursing rather than active or officious medication. In the first instance the animal should, if convenient, be removed to a loose box, with extra clothing, flannel bandages to the legs, deprivation of grain, warm mashes, and a small quantity of damped hay. If the running ·at the nose is considerable, the throat very sore, and the cough troublesome, it will be advisable to wrap several folds of thick flannel around the throat, which should be kept constantly wet with alcohol, or weak camphor and spirit — that is, one part camphor dissolved in sixteen parts alcohol. A dose of four drachms of either nitrate or sulphate of potass, dissolved in the drinking water, may be given once or twice each day. Active stimulants, particularly blisters, are wholly inadmissible. Demulcent drinks, such as linseed tea, hay tea, or oat or cornmeal, are useful and often acceptable. The animal should remain quiet in his box until all irritation in his throat has completely passed away. Even when the horse is " convalescent," the owner must not be in a hurry to get him into fast work, because the membrane of the larynx (upper portion of the windpipe) will continue to be for some time very susceptible of irritation and inflammation. In the advanced stages, if the debility is great and the appetite poor, much benefit is derived from the administration of tonics and stimulants. The following may be given daily: Iodide of iron one drachm, extract of gentian four drachms; mix for to make one ball, or dissolve in a pint of ale and then give as a drink. In cases, however, which are progressing favorably, Nature had better be left to herself, and tonics should only be resorted to when the symptoms really indicate the need of them.

DRESSING HOOF. — A good preparation, and one that will give the horse's hoof a rapid and healthy growth, is to take of oil of tar one pint, beeswax one and one-half pounds, whale oil four pints. The above ingredients should be mixed and melted together over a slow fire, and applied to all parts of the hoof at least once or twice a week.

EYE, INFLAMMATION OF. — Keep the horse quiet, and dress the eye repeatedly with the following lotion: Take of tincture of opium two ounces, and of water one pint; mix. Much depends upon a proper application of the lotion, and a most advantageous proceeding is to attach several folds of linen rag to the headstall so as to cover the eye, and by being repeatedly saturated it will keep up constant evaporation, as well as a cooling effect. The horse should also be removed from excessive light. When the inflammation has been subdued, the opacity — more or less of which is sure to remain — must be treated by the application of either iodide of potassium or nitrate of silver, prepared thus: Take of iodide of potassium twenty grains; water one ounce; mix; or take of nitrate of silver five grains; distilled water one ounce; mix. To be applied daily by means of a camel's-hair brush saturated with the lotion and drawn gently across the eye.

FARCY. — In most cases farcy is indicated by the appearance of one or more pustules, which break into a very peculiar, deep, abrupt ulcer, having thick inverted edges, which bleed freely on the slightest touch. The matter discharged from a farcy bud is either of a dirty, dingy yellow color or of a glue-like character; in either case it is offensive. Or it may be bloody or ichorous. In the latter case it abrades the surface on which it falls, or gravitates its regular corded lines into the cellular tissues, and hence it helps to spread the disease. In other cases this complaint commences with a very painful swelling of the hind leg, followed by the peculiar intractable ulcers described above. In treatment the horse should receive good care, fresh air, regular, moderate exercise, and be carefully kept apart from all others. Give daily in food for a fortnight two drachms of iodide of iron, four grains of canthafides, with two drachms each of powdered ginger and aniseed. The ulcers or sores should be dressed daily with carbolic acid.

FEET, HORSES', CARE OF. — Every person may see upon turning up the bottom of a horse's foot, an angular projection pointing towards the toe, termed the frog and its bars, the remainder or hollow part being technically called the sole, though the entire bottom of the foot might better receive this name. It is certain, however, that the " frog and sole " require pressure — a congenial kind of pressure without concussion — that shall cause the sensible, inside, or quicksole to perform its functions of absorbing the serous particles secreted or deposited therein by the blood vessels. If the frog and its bars are permitted to remain in such a state as to reach the ground, wherever the sod happens to be soft or yielding, the hollow part of the sole receives its due proportion of pressure laterally, and the whole sole or surface of the foot is thus kept in health.

Every veterinarian of sense will perceive the necessity of keeping the heels apart, yet though the immediate cause of their contracting is so universally known and recognized, the injudicious method — to call it by no harsher name — of paring away the frog and sole, which prevents the bars from ever touching the ground, is still continued to an alarming extent.

So much for prevention. When disease comes on, which may be accelerated by two other species of mismanagement, another course is usually followed not less injudicious than the first mentioned original cause of all the mischief.

Horses' hoofs are of two distinct kinds or shapes — the one being oval, hard, dark-colored, and thick; the other round, palish, and thin in the wall or crust of the hoof. The first has a different kind of frog from the latter, this being broad, thick and soft, while the oval hoof has a frog that is long, acute and hard. The rags, which hard work and frequent shoeing occasion on the horny hoof of the round foot, produce ragged frogs also, both being thus pared away to make a fair bottom to receive the shoe — burning hot! — the whole support is so far reduced, and the sensible sole coming much nearer the ground, becomes tender and liable to those painful concussions which bring on lameness — principally of the fore feet. Contraction of those kinds of heels which belong to the cart-horse, and pommice-foot, are the consequence.

The oval foot pertains to the saddle-horse, the hunter, and bit of blood-kind, whose bold projecting frogs the farriers remove, and these being compelled to perform long and painful journeys, ever starting or going off with the same leading leg, and continuing the same throughout, lameness is contracted in that foot, which none can account for, nor even find out whereabouts it may be seated. Applications of " the oyals " (that egregious compound of folly, ignorance, and brutality) follow the first appearance of this lameness, and are made alike to the shoulder, the leg, and the sole, under the various pretences of rheumatism, strain in the shoulder, and founder. The real cause, however, is not once thought of, much less removed, but, on the contrary, the evil is usually augmented by removing the shoe and drawing the sole to the quick, perhaps, in search of suppostitious corns, surbatings, etc. — pretended remedies that were never known to cure, but which might have been all prevented by the simplest precautions that can be imagined. These are: —

1. Let the frog and sole acquire their natural thickness.
2. Lead off sometimes with one leg, sometimes with another.
3. Stuff the hollow of the hoofs (all four of them) with cow dung or tar ointment, changing it entirely once a day. In every case it is advisable that he be worked moderately, for it is useless to talk to the owners of horses about giving the afflicted animal an entire holiday at grass.

FEET, BRITTLE. — In a large majority of cases brittleness of hoof owes its origin to mismanagement of the feet, and especially to excessive moisture, the use of swabs, the bath-tub, etc. In all cases where the hoof is naturally brittle the feet should be kept dry rather than wet. If convenient, we would remove the shoes, and rasp the wall moderately short and round at its margin. Having cut the hair off short around the entire coronet, a little iodide of mercury ointment should be rubbed in. This will cause a rapid growth of horn. The horse should be kept during the day in a roomy box having a layer of tan or sawdust spread over the floor. When removed to his stall at night the feet should be washed clean, and, after being wiped dry, every part of the hoof should be freely anointed with the following composition: Take of oil of tar and beeswax of each four ounces, honey and beef suet of each two ounces, whale oil eight ounces; melt the beeswax and beef suet first, then add the honey and other ingredients, stirring the whole until nearly cold. All sousing of the feet must be avoided.

FEET, CONTRACTED. — Horses which stand nearly or quite the year round, sometimes from year to year in the stable, are apt to have the feet get into a dry and fevered condition, the hoof becomes dry, hard, and often contracted, frequently also very brittle, and the horse sometimes suffers lameness in consequence. One of the most effective means of remedying these difficulties, where the horse cannot be spared to be turned loose into pasture for quite a season, is in the spring, when the ground is breaking up, and the winter's frost disappearing, and no lasting freeze is to be apprehended, to have all the shoes taken off, and drive the horse daily, about business as usual, without them. The roads remain muddy and soft, usually, so that a horse may be thus driven daily for a period of three or four weeks, and a great improvement is effected in the feet in every respect.

FEET, TO PREVENT SNOW-BALLING. — Clean their hoofs well, then rub thoroughly with thick soap suds before going out in the snow.

FISTULA. — Make a free opening in the lowest part of the sac and inject it daily with a lotion containing 2 drachms of chloride of zinc to a pint of soft water.

FLIES ON HORSES. — As a preventive of horses being teased by flies, take two or three small handfuls of walnut leaves, upon which pour two or three quarts of cold water; let it infuse for one night, and pour the whole next morning into a kettle, and let it boil for a quarter of an hour. When it becomes cold it will be fit for use. No more is required than to moisten a sponge, and, before the horse goes out of the stable, let those parts which are most irritable be smeared over with the liquor — namely, between and upon the ears, the neck, the flanks, etc. Not only the lady or gentleman who rides out for pleasure will derive pleasure from the walnut leaves thus prepared, but the coachman, the wagoner, and all others who use horses during the summer. Or take smart weed and soak it in water, and in the morning apply it to the horse, all over him, with a sponge. A decoction of quassia chips, made by boiling them in water, has also been recommended.

FRACTURE. — Severe lameness is sometimes caused by the fracture of one or two bones on the inside of the hoof — namely, the coffin of the navicular bone. Inclosed as these bones are on the inside of the hoof, and fenced in laterally by the cartilages, it is often difficult to detect, and we are obliged to depend on the general symptoms: the horse halts exceedingly, the foot is hot, and the pain extreme. As these bones are confined in the hoof no displacement can take place, therefore no *crepitus* can be detected. In all cases of fracture of either bone, a careful examination will, however, reveal the existence of a swelling at the back of the heels, immediately above the frog, and more or less fulness over the coronet of the foot. The treatment may be indicated in a few words — rest, absolute rest, is all-important. So long as the horse exhibits evidence of acute pain whenever his weight is imposed on the lame limb, the quieter he is kept the better. Warm baths, or cloths frequently moistened with a mixture of equal parts of alcohol and water, are useful adjuncts. It may be added that, in all cases of serious injury of the stifle, the hip-joint, or the pelvis, the horse is able to bring his heels " fair and square " upon the floor. In fracture of either the navicular or coffin bone, lameness sometimes continues long after recovery. It may turn out permanent.

FOOT. PUMMICE. — This is indicated by the hoofs spreading more and more, and losing their shape. A properly constructed round (bar) shoe is the only reliable remedy, for it can be worn indefinitely without detriment to any part of the foot. The main object of treatment is to protect and preserve the deformed sole. The shoe must be chambered so as not to touch the sole, and no paring away of the latter must be allowed. Keep the feet clean and dry as possible.

FOOT, SAND CRACK IN. — This, as its name imports, is a crack or division of the hoof from above downward, and into which sand and dirt are too apt to insinuate themselves. It occurs both in the fore and the hind feet. In the fore feet it is usually found in the inner quarter, but occasionally in the outer quarter, because there is the principal stress or effort towards expansion in the foot, and the inner quarter is not so strong as the outer. In the hind feet the crack is almost invariably found in the front, because in the digging of the toe into the ground, in the act of drawing, the principal stress is in front. If the crack be superficial — does not penetrate through the horn — it will cause no lameness, yet must not be neglected. If the crack has extended to the sensible parts, and you can see any fungus flesh, with a small drawing knife remove the edges of the cracked horn that press upon it. Touch the fungus with caustic, dip a roll of tow or linen in tar, and bind it very firmly over it. The whole foot is to be kept in a bran poultice for a few days, or until the lameness is removed. A shoe may then be put on, so as not to press on the diseased part. The pledget of tow may now be removed, the crack filled with composition, and the animal may be then turned into some soft meadow.

FOUNDER, TO CURE. — Clean out the bottom of the foot thoroughly, hold up firmly in a horizontal position, and pour in a tablespoonful of spirits of turpentine, if the cavity will hold that much ; if not, pour in what it will hold without running over ; touch the turpentine with a red-hot iron (this will set it on fire); hold the hoof firmly in this position till it burns out, and care must be taken that none runs on the hair of the hoof, lest the skin be burned. If all the feet are affected, burn turpentine in all of them. Relief will speedily follow, and the animal will be ready for service in a short time. Second. The seeds of the sunflower — a pint of the whole seed — given in his feed, immediately the founder is discovered. — Third. By standing the foundered horse up to his belly in water.

GALLED BACK. — So soon as an abrasion is discovered on the back of a horse, the animal should be excused from duty for a few days ; the abraded parts should be dressed twice daily with a portion of the tincture of aloes and myrrh. This simple treatment will soon heal the parts. Should there be no abrasion, but simply a swelling attended with heat, pain and tenderness, the parts should be frequently sponged with cold water. Occasionally the skin undergoes the process of hardening (induration). This is a condition of the parts, known to the farriers of old as " sitfast," and the treatment is as follows: Procure one ounce of iodine, and smear the indurated spot with a portion of the same twice daily. Some cases of galled back and shoulders are due to negligence and abuse ; yet many animals, owing to a peculiarity of constitution, will chafe, as the saying is, in those parts which come in contact with the collar, and neither human foresight nor mechanical means can prevent the same.

GLANDERS. — Glanders is a disease of very malignant type, and consists in a discharge from one or both nostrils of matter which, by transfer or inoculation, will produce the disease in any other animal. It is also characterized by tumefaction of the submaxillary and lymphatic glands. The lymphatic glands enlarge, a pustular eruption appears upon the skin, followed by suppurating, bloody, gangrenous ulceration in various parts, giving rise to small tumors, known as farcy buds. These gradually suppurate, and secrete a specific virus. The physiology and pathology of it is this: It occurs under two forms — namely, glanders and farcy. Many veterinarians have considered these varieties to be distinct diseases, but numerous experiments have demonstrated that they have their origin in the common animal poison. It appears, however, that there are two grades or varieties of this disease. Thus, if glanders be defined to be a disorder with a running of matter from the nose, enlargement and induration of the glands, farcy consists in the formation of a number of tumors on different parts of the body, which soften and ulcerate. It may be shortly stated that, in the primary stage of glanders, the nasal passages especially suffer, while in farcy it is the lymphatic system which is first affected. The catalogue of remedies proposed is endless. Sulphate of copper, sulphate of iron, cantharides, arsenic, and recently sulphate of soda and carbolic acid, have been used, but without benefit, and to the disappointment of the hopes which had been entertained of them. The disease is pronounced incurable by standard authorities, and an animal having it should be killed, rather than experimented on.

GRAVEL. — Steep one-half pound of hops in a quart of water, and give it as hot as the horse can stand it.

GRESE. — This is a white, offensive discharge from the skin of the heels. Wash the part well with warm soapsuds twice a day, and if the swelling be great, apply a poultice to it ; when the sores are cleansed, touch them with a rag or feather dipped

4*

in a solution of chloride of zinc, one grain to the ounce of water.

HAIR, LOSS OF.— To promote the growth of hair, where the skin has been deadened by bruises or rubbing, take of quinine eight grains, finely powdered galls ten grains, powdered capsicum five grains, oil of almonds and pure lard of each one ounce, oil of lavender twenty drops ; mix thoroughly, and apply a small quantity to the denuded parts two or three times a week. Where there is falling out of the hair of the mane and tail, take glycerine two ounces, sulphur one ounce, acetate of lead two drachms, water eight ounces. To be well mixed, and applied by means of a sponge.

HALTER–PULLING.— A new way to prevent horses pulling at the halter, is to put a very small rope under the horse's tail, bringing the ends forward, crossing them on the back, and tying them on the breast. Put the halter strap through the ring, and tie to the rope in front of the breast. When the horse pulls, he will, of course, find himself in rather an uncomfortable position, and discontinue the effort to free himself.

HARNESS, CARE OF.— First take the harness apart, having each strap and piece by itself, and then wash it in warm soapsuds. When it has been cleaned, black every part with the following dye: one ounce extract of logwood, 12 grains of bichromate of potash, both pounded fine; put it into two quarts of boiling rain water, and stir until all is dissolved. When cool it may be used. You can bottle and keep for future use if you wish. It may be applied with a shoe-brush, or anything else convenient. When the dye has struck in, you may oil each part with winter strained lard oil, dissolving in the oil (by gentle heat) one ounce of paraffine to one pint of oil, or the same amount of paraffine candle will answer, applied with a paint-brush, or anything convenient. A few hours after wipe clean with a woollen cloth, which gives the harness a glossy appearance. The preparation will not injure the leather or stitching, makes it soft and pliable, and obviates the necessity of oiling as often as is necessary by the ordinary method.

HARNESS OR BOOT POLISH, VERY FINE.— Put half a pound of gum shellac, broken up in small pieces, in a quart bottle or jug; cover it with alcohol, cork it tight, and put it on a shelf in a warm place; shake it well several times a day, then add a piece of gum camphor as large as a hen's egg; shake it well, and in a few hours shake it again, and add one ounce of lampblack; if the alcohol is good, it will be dissolved in three days;

then shake and use.  If it gets too thick, add alcohol — pour out two or three teaspoonfuls in a saucer, and apply it with a small paint brush.  If the materials are all good, it will dry in about five minutes, and will be removed only by wearing it off, giving a gloss almost equal to patent leather.  The advantage of this preparation above others is, it does not strike into the leather and make it hard, but remains on the surface, and yet excludes the water almost perfectly.  This same preparation is admirable for harness, and this does not soil when touched, as lamp-black preparations do.

HEAVES.—This disease is indicated by a short, dull, spasmodic cough, and a double-jerking movement at the flank during expiration.  If a horse suffering from this disease is allowed to distend his stomach at his pleasure, with dry food entirely, and then to drink cold water, as much as he can hold, he is nearly worthless.  But if his food be moistened, and he be allowed to drink a moderate quantity only at a time, the disease is much less troublesome.  To cure this complaint, feed no hay to the horse for thirty-six or forty-eight hours, and give only a pailful of water at a time.  Then throw an armful of well cured smart weed before him, and let him eat all he will.  Great relief, if not a perfect cure, will follow.  Another remedy is sunflower seed, feeding one or two quarts of the seed daily.

HIDE-BOUND.—To recruit a hide-bound horse, give nitrate potassia (or saltpetre) four ounces, crude antimony one ounce, sulphur three ounces.  Nitrate of potassia and antimony should be finely pulverized, then add the sulphur, and mix the whole well together.  Dose—A tablespoonful of this mixture in a bran mash daily.

HOOF-BOUND.—Cut down several lines from the coronet to the toe all around the hoof, and fill the cuts with tallow and soap mixed; take off the shoes, and (if you can spare him) turn the animal into a wet meadow, where his feet will be kept moist.  Never remove the sole nor burn the lines down, as this increases instead of diminishing the evil.

## HORSE MEDICINES.

DR. COLE'S KING OF OILS.—1 oz. green copperas; 2 oz. white vitriol; 2 oz. common salt; 2 oz. linseed oil; 8 oz. molasses.  Boil over a slow fire fifteen minutes, in a pint of urine; when almost cold, add 1 oz. of oil of vitriol and 4 oz. of spirits turpentine.  Apply to wounds with a feather.  A very powerful liniment.

MEXICAN MUSTANG LINIMENT. — Petroleum, olive oil. and carbonate of ammonia. each equal parts; and mix. It is one of the best liniments in use.

MERCHANT'S GARGLING OIL. — Take 2½ gals. linseed oil; 2½ gals. spirits turpentine; 1 gal. Western petroleum; 8 oz. liquor potass; sap green, 1 oz. Mix all together and it is ready for use.

ARABIAN CONDITION POWDERS. — Ground ginger, 1 lb.; sulphuret of antimony, 1 lb.; powdered sulphur, 1 lb.; saltpetre, 1 lb. Mix all together; and administer in a mash, in such quantities as may be required. The best condition powder in existence.

BLISTERING LINIMENT. — 1 part Spanish flies, finely powdered; 3 of lard; and 1 of yellow rosin. Mix the lard and rosin together, and add the flies when the other ingredients begin to cool. To render it more active, add one pint spirits turpentine.

FOR STRAINS AND SWELLINGS. — Strong vinegar saturated with common salt, used warm, is good for strains and reducing swellings. 1 oz. of white vitriol; 1 oz. of green copperas; 2 teaspoonfuls of gunpowder, all pulverized together, and dissolved in 1 quart of soft water, and used cold, rubbing in thoroughly, is one of the best applications known for reducing swellings.

HOOF-BOUND WASH. — Spirits of turpentine, 4 oz.; tar, 4 oz.; whale-oil, 8 oz. Mix, and apply to the hoofs often.

HOOFS, TO TOUGHEN. — Wash them frequently in strong brine, and turn brine upon the bottoms, and soak a few minutes each time.

COUGH. — Quit feeding musty hay, and feed roots and laxative food. Sprinkle human urine on his fodder, or cut up cedar boughs and mix with his grain; or boil a small quantity of flaxseed, and mix it in a mash of scalded bran, adding a few ounces of sugar, molasses, or honey. Administer lukewarm. If there should be any appearance of *heaves*, put a teaspoonful of ground ginger once per day, in his provender, and allow him to drink freely of lime water.

COLIC CURE. — Bleed freely at the horse's mouth; then take ¼ lb. raw cotton, wrap it around a coal of fire, so as to exclude the air; when it begins to smoke, hold it under his nose till he becomes easy.

To Cure Distemper. — Take 1¼ gals. of blood from the neck vein; then administer sassafras oil, 1½ ounces. Cure, speedy and certain.

Founder Cured in 24 Hours. — Boil or steam stout oat-straw for half an hour, then wrap it around the horse's leg quite hot, cover up with wet woollen rags to keep in the steam; in 6 hours renew the application. take 1 gal. of blood from the neck vein, and give one quart linseed oil. He may be worked next day.

Cure for Staggers. — Give a mess twice a week, composed of bran, 1 gal.; sulphur, 1 table-teaspoonful; saltpetre, 1 spoonful; boiling sassafras tea, 1 quart; assafœtida, 1⅛ oz. Keep the horse from cold water for half a day afterwards.

Ring–Bone and Spavin. — Take sweet oil, 4 oz.; spirits turpentine, 2 oz.; oil of stone, 1 oz. Mix, and apply three times per day. If the horse is over four years old, or in any case when this is not sufficient, in addition to it, you will fit a bar of lead just above it, wiring the ends together, so it constantly wears upon the enlargement; and the two together will cure nine cases out of every ten, in six weeks.

To Tame Horses. — Take finely-grated horse castor, oils of rhodium and cummin; keep them in separate bottles well-corked; put some of the oil cummin on your hand, and approach the horse on the windy side. He will then move towards you. Then rub some of the cummin on his nose, give him a little of the castor on anything he likes, and get eight or ten drops oil rhodium on his tongue. You can then get him to do anything you like. Be kind and attentive to the animal, and your control is certain.

Best Remedy for Heaves. — Balsam of fir and balsam of copaiba, 4 oz. each, and mix with calcined magnesia sufficiently thick to make it into balls; and give a middling-sized ball night and morning for a week or ten days.

Cure for Bots in Horses. — Give the horse first, 2 quarts of new milk, and 1 quart molasses, fifteen minutes afterwards, give 2 quarts very strong sage tea; 30 minutes after the tea, give 3 pints (or enough to operate as physic) of curriers' oil. The molasses and milk cause the bots to let go their hold, the tea puckers them up, and the oil carries them completely away. Cure certain, in the worst cases.

Certain Ring-bone and Spavin Cure. — Venice turpentine and Spanish flies, of each 2 oz.; euphorbium and aqua-ammonia, of each 1 oz.; red precipitate, ½ oz.; corrosive sublimate, ¼ oz.; lard, 1½ lbs. Pulverize all, and put into the lard; simmer slowly over coals, not scorching or burning; and pour off, free of sediment. For ring-bones, cut off the hair, and rub the ointment well into the lumps once in forty-eight hours For spavins, once in twenty-four hours for three mornings. Wash well previous to each application with suds, rubbing over the place with a smooth stick to squeeze out a thick, yellow matter. This has removed very large ring-bones.

BONE SPAVINS, FRENCH PASTE. — $300 RECIPE. — Corrosive sublimate, quicksilver, and iodine, of each 1 oz. Rub the quicksilver and iodine together; then add the sublimate, and lastly the lard, rubbing them thoroughly. Shave off the hair the size of the bone enlargement; grease all around it, but not where the hair is shaved off: this prevents the action of the medicine, except on the spavin. Then rub in as much of the paste as will lic on a three-cent piece, each morning, for three or four mornings. In from seven to eight days, the whole spavin will come out; then wash the wound with suds for an hour or so, to remove the poisonous effects of the paste; afterwards heal up the sore with any good healing salve, or Sloan's Horse Ointment, as per recipe above, keeping the sore covered while it is healing up.

ANOTHER VERY VALUABLE RECIPE FOR RING-BONE. — Pulverized cantharides, oils of spike, origanum, amber, cedar, Barbadoes tar, and British oil, of each 2 oz.; oil of wormwood, 1 oz.; spirits turpentine, 4 oz.: common potash, ½ oz.: nitric acid, 6 oz.; sulphuric acid, 4 oz.; lard 3 lbs. Melt the lard, and slowly add the acids; stir well, and add the other articles, stirring till cold; clip off the hair, and apply by rubbing and heating in. In about three days, or when it is done running, wash off with soapsuds and apply again. In old cases, it may take three or four weeks, but in recent cases, two or three applications have cured.

ANOTHER. — Pulverized cantharides, oils of origanum and amber, and spirits turpentine, of each 1 oz.; olive oil, ½ oz.; sulphuric acid, 3 drachms; put all except the acid, into alcohol; stir the mixture, add the acid slowly, and continue to stir till the mixture ceases to smoke; then bottle for use. Apply to ring-bone or spavin with a sponge tied on the end of a stick, as long as it is absorbed into the parts; twenty-four hours after, grease well with lard; and in twenty-four hours more, wash off well with soap-suds. One application is generally sufficient for spavins, but may need two; ring-bones, always two or three applications, three or four days apart, which prevents loss of hair. This will stop all lameness but does not remove the lump.

SPLINT AND SPAVIN LINIMENT. — Oil of origanum, 6 oz.; gumcamphor, 2 oz.; mercurial ointment, 2 oz.; iodine ointment, 1 oz.; melt by putting all into a wide-mouthed bottle, and setting it in a kettle of hot water. Apply it to bone spavins or splints, twice daily for four or five days, and a cure is guaranteed.

LINIMENT FOR SWEENY. — Alcohol and spirits turpentine of each, 8 oz.; camphor-gum, pulverized cantharides, and capsicum, of each, 1 oz.; oil of spike, 3 oz.; mix. Bathe this liniment in with a hot iron, and a certain cure is sure to follow.

FOR LOOSENESS OR SCOURING IN HORSES OR CATTLE. — Tormentil root powdered. Dose for a horse or cow, 1 to $1\frac{1}{2}$ oz. It may be stirred into 1 pint of milk, and given; or it may be steeped in $1\frac{1}{2}$ pints of milk, then given from three to six times daily, until cured.

SCOURS AND PIN-WORMS IN HORSES AND CATTLE. — White ash bark burnt into ashes, and made into a rather strong lye; then mix $\frac{1}{2}$ pint of it with 1 pint warm water, and give all two or three times daily. This will certainly carry off the worms, which are the cause, in most instances, of scours and looseness.

ENGLISH STABLE LINIMENT, VERY STRONG. — Oil of spike, aqua-ammonia, and *oil* of turpentine, each 2 oz.; sweet oil, and oil of amber, each $1\frac{1}{2}$ oz.; oil of origanum, 1 oz.   Mix.

COLIC CURE FOR HORSES. — Spirits turpentine, 3 oz.; laudanum, 1 oz.; mix; and for a horse give all for a dose, by putting it into a bottle with half a pint of warm water. If relief is not obtained in an hour, repeat the dose, adding half an ounce of the best powdered aloes, well dissolved. Cure certain.

LINIMENT FOR FIFTY CENTS PER GALLON. — Best vinegar, 2 quarts; pulverized saltpetre, $\frac{1}{2}$ lb.; mix, and set in a cool place till dissolved. Invaluable for old swellings, sprains, bruises, etc.

SADDLE AND HARNESS GALLS, etc. — White lead and linseed oil, mixed as for paint, is almost unrivalled for healing saddle, harness, or collar galls and bruises. Try it, applying with a brush. It soon forms an air-tight coating, and soothes the pain, powerfully assisting nature.

GREASE HEEL. — Lye made from wood-ashes, and boil white

oak bark in it till it is quite strong, both in lye and bark-ooze; when it is cold, it is fit for use. Wash off the horse's leg with Castile soap; when dry. apply the above lye with a swab fastened on a long stick to keep out of his reach, as the smart caused by the application might make him let fly without much warning; but it is a sure cure, only it brings off the hair. To restore the hair after the cure is effected, make and apply a salve by stewing elder bark in old bacon; then form the salve by adding a little resin, according to the amount of oil when stewed, or $\frac{1}{4}$ lb. resin to each pound of oil.

VALUABLE REMEDY FOR HEAVES. — Calcined magnesia, balsam of fir, balsam copaiba, of each 1 oz.; spirits turpentine, 2 oz.; put them all into 1 pint best cider vinegar; give for a dose, 1 tablespoonful in his feed, once a day for a week; then every other day for two or three months. Wet his hay with brine, and also his other feed. He will cough more at first, but looser and looser till cured.

To DISTINGUISH AND CURE DISTEMPER. — Wet up bran with rather strong lye; if not too strong, the horse will eat it greedily. If they have the distemper, a free discharge from the nostrils, and a consequent cure will be the result, if continued a few days; but, if only a cold, with swelling of the glands, no change will be discovered.

REMEDY FOR FOUNDER. — Draw about a gallon blood from the neck; then drench the horse with linseed oil, 1 quart; now rub the fore-legs long and well with water as hot as can be borne without scalding.

PHYSIC FOR CATTLE. — Take *half* only of the dose above for a horse, and add to it glauber-salts, 8 oz.; dissolve all in gruel, 1 quart, and give as a drench.

. BLISTER, LIQUID. — Take $\frac{1}{2}$ a pint of linseed oil, 1 pint of spirits of turpentine, and 4 oz. of aqua ammonia; shake well and it is fit for use. Apply every third hour until it blisters.

BIG LEG.— To cure, apply the above Liquid Blister every third hour until it blisters. In three days wash the leg with linseed oil. In six days wash it clean with soap and water. Repeat every six days until the swelling goes down. If there should be any callous left, apply spavin ointment.

BIG HEAD.— When this disease occurs, every care must be devoted to improving the general health. Let work be regular and moderate.  Have the stable clean, dry, and well ventilated. Feed on sound hay and oats, either bruised or cooked.  Withhold all Indian corn — above all if raw and hard.  4 or 5 lbs. or linseed cake may be given daily.  Give every day, in the feed, 2

BALSAM, WOUND.— Gum benzoin in powder 6 oz. balsam of sam of tolu in powder 3 oz., gum storax 2 oz., frankincense in powder 2 oz., gum myrrh in powder 2 oz., socotorine aloes in powder 3 oz., alcohol 1 gal.  Mix them all together and put them in a digester, and give them a gentle heat for three or four days, and then strain.

BALL, COUGH — Pulverized ipecac $\frac{3}{4}$ of an oz., camphor 2 oz. squills $\frac{1}{2}$ an oz.  Mix with honey to form into mass, and didvide into 8 balls.  Give 1 every morning.

BALLS, DIURETIC.— Castile soap scraped fine, and powdered rosin, each 3 teaspoonfuls; powdered nitre 4 teaspoonfuls, oil of juniper 1 small teaspoonful, honey a sufficient quantity to make into a ball.

BALLS, FEVER.— Emetic tartar and camphor each $\frac{1}{2}$ oz., and nitre 2 oz.  Mix with linseed meal and molasses to make eight balls, and give one twice a day.

BALL, PHYSIC.— Take 2 oz., of aloes, 1 oz., of turpentine, and 1 oz., of flour; make into a paste with a few drops of water, wrap in a paper, and give them with a bailing iron.

BALL, PURGATIVE.— Aloes 1 oz., cream tartar and Castile soap $\frac{1}{4}$ oz.  Mix with molasses to make a ball.

BALL, WORM.— Assafetida 4 oz., gentian 2 oz., strong mercurial ointment 1 oz.  Make into mass with honey.  Divide into sixteen balls.  Give one or more every morning.

BAULKY HORSES, TO CURE.— A man, in order to be able to control a horse, must first learn to control himself.  One method to cure a baulky horse is to take him from the carriage, and whirl him rapidly round till he is giddy.  It requires two men to accomplish this — one at the horse's tail.  Don't let him step out.  Hold him to the smallest possible circle.  One dose will often cure him; two doses are final with the worst horse that ever refused to stir.  Another is to fill his mouth with dirt or gravel from the road, and he will at once go — the philosophy of this being that it gives him something else to think of.

# DOMESTIC ANIMALS.

ANIMALS, EFFECT OF KINDNESS ON. — The efficacy of the soothing word, the gentle touch, has only to be honestly tried to be fully appreciated. It may be set down as a fixed fact that whenever a horse or a cow or an ox is timid and shy — will not allow a person to approach or handle, unless it is so situated that it cannot escape — a wrong system of treatment has been pursued. The animals of the farmer are naturally disposed to be docile and affectionate. They recognize the voice and hand of a friend almost as soon as a human being would, and manifest their affection in a variety of ways, which none but the kind master or keeper will observe. Have you not seen teamsters who could manage their teams by a soft word far better than others could do by blows and harsh words? Animals almost invariably partake of the character of their masters. The kind, gentle and considerate master will generally have kind, gentle animals; while the rude, impetuous and cruel master will rarely fail to have animals whose dispositions will mate with his own. Is not gentleness the true method?

## CATTLE.

CATTLE, AGE OF, HOW TO TELL. — The age of the ox or cow is told chiefly by the teeth, and less perfectly by the horns. The temporary teeth are in part through at birth, and all the incisors are through in twenty days; the first, second, and third pairs of molars are through in thirty days; the teeth have grown large enough to touch each other by the sixth month; they gradually wear and fall in eighteen months; the fourth permanent molars are through at the fourth month; the fifth at the fifteenth month; the sixth at two years. The temporary teeth begin to fall at twenty-one months, and are entirely replaced by the thirty-ninth to the forty-fifth month. The development is quite complete at from five to six years. At that time the border of the incisors has been worn a little below the level of the grinders. At six years the first grinders are beginning to wear, and are on a level with the incisors. At eight years the wear of the first grinders is very apparent. At ten or eleven years, used surfaces of the teeth bear a square mark, surrounded by a white line; and this is perceived on all the teeth by the twelfth year; between the twelfth and the fourteenth year, this mark takes a round form. The rings on the horns are less useful as guides. At ten or twelve months the first ring appears; at twenty months to two years the second; at thirty to thirty-two months the third; at forty to forty-six months the fourth; at fifty-four to sixty months the fifth ring, and so on. But, at the fifth year, the three first rings are indistinguishable, and at the eighth year all the rings; besides, the dealers file the horns.

CATTLE, CATARRH IN. — Malignant catarrh, or coryza, has been confounded with the cattle plague or rinderpest, in some point of which there is a resemblance. *Symptoms.* — In first stage, a shivering fit may be observed; dulness, head held low, ears pendulous, the visible membranes of which are of a bluish-red color and dry; eyes closed and swollen, tears flow, and light cannot be endured; muzzle dry and hot, saliva discharged abundantly; painful cough, pulse frequent and full, heart's action feeble, bowels costive, feces black and hard, but after a short time diarrhea ensues; urine scanty, offensive, and of a high color; is thirsty, but eats nothing. The second stage occurs within eighteen or twenty-four hours from the appearance of the first signs of disturbance, and is denoted by a very marked change in the character of the discharges. The membranes of the eyes and nose now furnish a purulent secretion, having an admixture of blood and ichor, which irritates and makes sore the skin over which it flows. Within the sinuses of the head large accumulations of pus occur, and when the bones over them are tapped by the fingers (percussed) a dull sound is emitted. If the mouth is opened, red patches will be observed, which in some places will have fallen off, exposing a foul ulcer beneath, and the membranes are now of a deeper purple hue, and the breath fetid. The animal is lame, and experiences great pain when urine or dung is discharged. Pregnant animals are almost sure to cast their young (abort). In the third stage great prostration is evident. Sloughing of membranes extensive, and probably the horns and hoofs have come off. The pulse has become imperceptible, and convulsions ensue, with general coldness. The thermometer indicates a rapid and unusual fall, ninety to ninety-five degrees F. being the amount of heat that can be registered at the rectum. Sometimes ulceration of the cornea is effected before death, and the contents of the eyeball discharged, giving rise to a great amount of additional pain. *Duration.* — From four to nine or eleven days. *Treatment.* — Remove the animal from the pasture, and place it in a comfortable, cool place, with good bedding. Cooling or evaporating lotions, water, etc., should be constantly applied to the head. Injections of warm water should be thrown up. The following laxative drink may be administered: —

Take of Epsom salts twelve pounds, ground ginger two ounces, treacle one-half pound, and warm ale one and one-half pints. Mix and give to a two year old beast; three-quarters for one year old; one-half at six months, and one-quarter for lesser animals, as calves, sheep. and large pigs. Two or four drachms of nitre in water may be given three or four times a day. Solutions of carbolic acid, or sulphurous acid gas and chlorine in water, should be used for the purpose of dressing the wounds and cleansing the points of discharge. etc. It may also be necessary to open the sinuses and sponge them, using the same solutions.

CATTLE, CHOKED, TO RELIEVE. — In choking, the accumulation of gas (chiefly sulphuretted hydrogen) is the cause of the animal's death. This gas can be decomposed by the forcing of chloride of lime down the animal's throat. A strong solution of salt and water will also effect the same object. Another mode of relief is to force the animal to jump over the bars of a gate or fence, as high as she will jump, and when she touches ground on the opposite side the obstruction will be ejected. Another plan is to take a loaded gun, slip up by the side of the animal, place the muzzle directly between the horns, about three inches forward of them, and discharge the piece. A sudden spring of the animal backward results, and the obstruction is removed. And yet another is to use four or five feet of three-quarter rubber hose, and push the obstruction down.

CATTLE, BLACK LEG IN. — This can be cured by thoroughly washing the diseased leg in strong soap suds; rub till dry; then scrape the knots with a dull knife; then take one ounce of vitriol and dissolve in strong vinegar, after which the leg must be very thoroughly bathed and dried.

. CATTLE, FEEDING AND CARE OF. — The two great points in the feeding of cattle are regularity and a particular care to the weaker individuals. On this last account there ought to be plenty of rack or trough room, that too many may not feed together; in which very common case the weaker are not only trampled down by the stronger, but they are worried, cowed and spiritless; than which there cannot be a more unfavorable state for thrift; beside, they are ever compelled to shift with the worst of the fodder. To prevent this, the weaker animals should be kept and fed apart. The barn or stable should be kept warm in winter. During the winter months, whenever the sun shines, turn them into the yard, and they will soon find the sunny side, and begin to stretch themselves and show increased comfort. A good plan is to feed them meal or roots early in the morning, without any hay, and turn them out a little after sunrise, and then feed hay, either in the yard or at the adjoining stack, putting them back in the stalls as early as 4 P. M., stormy or extreme cold weather excepted, when they should be kept comfortably housed the most of the time. *In fattening*, the farmer should remember that it does not pay to feed grain to a poor creature — one that does not take on flesh rapidly. This kind of stock should at once be disposed of for what it will bring. The next important point is to feed plentifully, without stint, and to do this regularly and not too often, as the stock will eat and lie down and ruminate.

CATTLE, FILM ON EYES OF. — To remove it, apply clean lard, warm or cold, whichever way it can be got into the eye best. Its application will cause no pain, and should be applied until the film is removed. Another method is to apply powdered sugar.

CATTLE, FOOT AND MOUTH DISEASE IN. — On the first indication of this disease, the affected cattle should at once be separated from the healthy, so as to secure against the spreading of the disorder. Next make a mixture composed of five pounds of alum to twelve gallons of soft water, four quarts of salt, and a small quantity of tar, and with a sponge or rag wash the inside of the mouths thoroughly of those not affected. Next bathe the lower portion of the legs with suds formed from carbolic disinfecting soap, to which is added one quart of salt, to about one gallon of suds. Repeat the bathing and washing once a day for seven days. The affected animals should be treated in the same manner with the exception of washing the inside of the mouth twice a day — once with the mixture given above, and once with wormwood steeped in vinegar. To the division of the hoof apply suds at first, and afterwards apply a mixture of pitch and tar. The buildings should be thoroughly disinfected by carbolic acid, chloride of lime, and other disinfectants, and if the cattle themselves be treated with the fumes of burning sulphur, it will help to prevent further infection, for which purpose drop small pieces of brimstone upon live coals, contained in suitable metallic vessels (so as to avoid all risk of communicating fire), and allow the fumes to mingle with the air of the lean-to, or building containing the cattle, and to penetrate the coats of the beasts, and to be inhaled to such extent as can be borne by the attendant without serious discomfort. Let this be regularly repeated, daily or twice daily while the danger continues, using from one to two ounces each time, according to the extent of the danger.

Finally, the animals should be kept in a dry, comfortable place, suitably ventilated, and receive good nursing, including the utmost cleanliness. No bleeding must be allowed, nor should active purgatives be given them. If unable to take their usual food, their strength should be sustained by giving mashes of coarse-ground wheat, with bran, or other similar diet.

CATTLE, HOOF ROT IN. — For a cure, take one teacupful of sharp cider vinegar, one and one-half tablespoonfuls of copperas, one and one-half tablespoonfuls of salt. Dissolve gradually on the hot stove, but do not let it boil. When cool, apply it on the affected limb and hoof, and also swab out the mouth of the animal with the mixture. Two or three applications generally effect a cure. This preparation can be used in the foot and mouth disease in connection with the above treatment.

CATTLE, HOVEN OR BLOAT IN. — A certain remedy for this is to take a pail of water, fresh from the stream, and pour it from a jug forward of the hip bones, rubbing it on with the hands. It will be found that the bloat will at once commence to go down, and by applying two or three more pailfuls complete restoration will result.

CATTLE, LICE ON, TO DESTROY. — 1. Camphor dissolved in spirits, is an effectual remedy  2. One part lard and two parts coal oil, melted together and applied, will kill lice without fail. 3. A strong brine, thickened with soft soap will also kill. 4. Two or three applications of kerosene oil, applied by carding the animal, and dipping the teeth of the card in the oil, is convenient, harmless and effectual. 5. Feeding onions to the animal will make the lice travel in from ten to fifteen hours.

CATTLE, MANGE IN. — This is caused by improper treatment of the animal through the winter, rendering it debilitated and unable to support the change when the grass comes on. Nature, overloaded, will relieve herself by this eruption on the skin, which, once introduced, will quickly spread through an entire dairy. The treatment required is proper attention to cleanliness, food, drink, and plenty of sunlight.

CATTLE PLAGUE. — Chloride of copper is now extensively used in Germany as a preventive against the cattle plague. The mode of administering the specific is as follows: A solution is first made by dissolving one-quarter of an ounce of the green crystallized salts in spirits of wine. In this solution a pad of cotton is soaked for a little while, and is then laid on a plate and set on fire in the centre of the stable, the animals' heads being turned towards the flame, so as to make them breathe the fumes. The operation is performed morning and evening, and a spirit-lamp filled with the solution left burning in the stable every night. The liquid is also administered internally, with the addition of one-half an ounce of chloroform for the above quantity, a teaspoonful being put into the animal's drink three times a day.

CATTLE'S HORNS, SAWING OFF. — A celebrated professor of a London Veterinary College has said, concerning this practice: I consider this to be a very gross act of cruelty, and for this reason — that the horns of oxen are very unlike those of the deer species. They have a large proportion of bone growing out from the bone of the head, and that is surrounded by a heavy sensitive structure, so that to cut the animal's horns, they had to go below where it is simply horny, and the animal had to suffer much pain. The nearer the operation was performed to the skull, the greater the suffering. That bone was hollow — that is to say, it had not one single horned cavity — but it had several cells, which extended into the head, though not to the brain, but close to it. These cavities were exposed, by the removal of the horns, to the air ; and as they are lined with a delicate, sensitive membrane — there being, besides, a delicate, sensitive covering outside — great suffering must be caused. The cavities were never intended by Nature to be exposed to the air, which brought on an inflammatory condition. These cavities were very apt to be inflamed, and the inflammation was very likely to be extended to the membranes of the brain, causing madness, lockjaw. or other dangerous results. This operation is one of the most painful and unwarrantable that could possibly be performed on cattle.

CATTLE, SNAKE-BITTEN, REMEDY FOR. — Cattle or horses are usually bitten in the feet. When this is the case, all that is necessary to do is to drive them into a mudhole, and keep them there for a few hours ; if upon the nose, bind the mud upon the place, in such a manner as not to interfere with their breathing.

CATTLE, SORE MOUTH IN. — Take a weak solution of carbolic acid — say one to five drops to the ounce of water — washing the mouth every few hours, allowing a little to be swallowed, and following this with mild tonics, and food that will not irritate the mouth.

CATTLE, WARTS ON. — 1. To remove warts from cattle, mix equal parts of blue vitriol, lard and honey, and anoint them once in four or five days ; they will be removed without making a sore. 2. Wash with a strong lye made of pearl-ash and water three times a day.  3.  Or make two or three applications of lunar caustic.

Cows, Abortion in — The predisposing cause for this disease is constitutional in the animal, while the exciting cause may be ill-treatment at the time of pregnancy, damp surroundings, food in which ergot of rye may be found, impure water, etc.  The predisposing cause can be avoided by giving the generative organs of the animal a rest.  The doing of this, by a freedom of from six months to a year from pregnancy, will insure freedom from abortion — especially so if care is taken in the avoiding of all supposable exciting causes.  Many farmers may not be willing to endure the loss involved in this suggestion; but it will be a gain in the end, because no animal aborts without, in a greater or less measure experiencing such a shock to her system as will tell on her future health and value.

Cows, Care of. — 1.  Cows should run dry six weeks before calving ; if milked closely towards calving, the calves will be poorer.

2.  A cow newly come in should not drink cold water in cold weather, but moderately warm water.  Calves, intended for raising, should be taken from the cow within a few days, and they will be less liable to suck when they are old.  Feed them first on new milk, for a short time, and then on skim milk, taking care that all the changes are gradual, by adding only a portion at first.

3.  Hearty eaters are desirable for cows, and may usually be selected while calves.  A dainty calf will be a dainty cow.

4.  Heifers dried up too early after calving, will always run dry about the same time in after years — therefore, be careful to milk closely the first year, until about six weeks previous to the time for calving.

5.  Spring cows should come in while they are yet fed on hay, and before they are turned to grass, which will be more likely to prevent caked bag and milk fever.

6.  The best times for feeding the cow are early in the morning, at noon, and a little before sunset.

7.  Abundance of the purest water must always be supplied, and it ought in all cases, when practicable, be what is understood as soft water.  In winter the water given should be warmed to the temperature of the air on a summer day.

8.  The food given should be as nearly in its natural state as possible.  Cooking food, slops, brewers' grains, etc., are all objectionable, where either firm, healthy flesh, or pure, rich milk is desired.

Cows, Dairy, to Select.—Cows of extraordinary milking qualities are as often found among the natives as among grade and thoroughbred animals ; and, as a rule, the progeny of these extra-milkers become the best cows, and every heifer-calf from such should be raised, except it fails to carry the mark indicating a good milker. This mark is the upward growth of the hair on the inside of the thighs of the calf from immediately behind the udder, as high as the hair goes. If it be found running up in a very smooth and unbroken column—all the other things being equal—with good care and continued fine growth, there will scarcely be a failure. But whatever extraordinary qualities the cow may possess, unless this mark is found on the calf, it is not worth raising for a dairy cow. There are several other signs and conditions indicative of valuable milking qualities, some of which attend the first described. Smooth and fair-sized teats; a large and long milk vein ; slim neck; and sometimes six teats; a yellow skin, apparent about the eyes and nose, and other bare spots, are indications of rich milk, and one of the indications of a good cow.

Cows, Farrow, What to Do With.— Feed them liberally, and they will give rich milk, though, perhaps, not much of it. Let them have three or four quarts of meal a day through the winter and spring, and do not stop giving it to them when grass comes. As soon as it dries them up they will be fit for the butcher.

Cows, Bloody Milk in.— To cure, give a tablespoonful of milk in a little bran or meal, and renewing the dose the second or third day. Another remedy is to give a tablespoonful of sulphur in a little dry bran, once a day—in very bad cases, twice a day.

Cows, Garget in.—This disorder is very frequent in cows after ceasing to be milked : it affects the glands of the udder with hard swellings, and often arises from the animal not being clean milked. It may be removed by giving a pint of beans a day, for four or five days. The beans should be soaked and mixed with meal to make the cow eat them ; but the better way is to grind the beans, and feed a pint a day with other meal. This will be found a sure remedy. Another plan is to give the cow one teaspoonful of the tincture of arnica, in bran or shorts, three times a day, and bathe the bag thoroughly with it as often. The arnica for bathing should be reduced one-half in warm water, and bathe with the hand.

Cows, Hard-Milking.— The causes for cows holding up

their milk are various — irregularity in time of milking, imperfect milking, and lack of water in pastures ; over-driving in bringing the animals home ; the taking of the calf away — and especially will this be the case where the calf, while being reared, is kept in a situation where the mother can keep up an acquaintance with it ; and finally the presence of a vicious or sulky disposition in the cow, the slightest dissatisfaction making them hold up their milk.  The remedy in usual cases is, besides the avoidance of the apparent cause, gentleness, kind words, and a system of petting the animals, so as to gain their confidence and affection, coupled with plenty of good water and feed.

Cows, Kicking. — Cows seldom kick without some good reason for it.  Teats sometimes are chapped or the udder tender ; harsh handling hurts them, and they kick.  Sometimes long and sharp fingernails cut their teats, and sometimes the milker pulls the long hairs on the udder, while milking.  Shear off the long hairs, cut long finger-nails close, bathe chapped teats with warm water, and grease them well with lard, and always treat a cow gently.  She never will kick unless something hurts her, or she fears a repetition of former hurts.  When handled gently cows like to be milked.  When treated otherwise, they will kick and hold up their milk.  Occasionally a cow is found that, like some men, has a bad, ungovernable temper, that flies at merely imaginary offences.  For this class take a small strap long enough for the purpose, and bend the foreleg so as to bring the foot up to the body.  Then put the strap round the arm and small part of the leg, near the hoof, crossing between, so as not to slip off over the knee, and buckle.  In this condition, it is an impossibility for a cow to kick ; they may come to the knee, a few times, but are soon quiet.  Never, as some do, confine the hind legs, either singly or together, for in doing this there is danger of spoiling the animal.  Milkers should study the temper of the cows they milk, and find out whether a cow kicks on account of pain or wilfulness.  If it is from bad temper, the strap applied to the foot is a very good way to subdue her, but you should avoid whipping and beating in all cases.

Cows, Rheumatism in. — The treatment of rheumatism should consist in placing the animal in a moderately warm place, and giving diet of a generous character.  In cases where the pain is severe, the tincture of aconite, in twenty drop doses, may be given with advantage.  Friction to the joints will be found beneficial ; and, where much swelling exists, the liniment of ammonia may be rubbed in daily.  Cooling appliances do not seem to suit this complaint.  The enlargements in the joints sometimes become chronic, and should then be treated with applications of the tincture of iodine.

**COWS, MILKING, THE RIGHT METHOD OF.**— Some persons in milking seize the root of the teat between the thumb and forefinger, and then drag upon it until it slips out of their grasp. In this way teat and udder are subjected to severe traction for an indefinite number of times, and in rude hands are often severely injured. Others, again, by carelessness and want of thoroughness, will cause the usual quantity of milk to shrink one-third in two weeks. In many localities more cows are ruined from faults of bad milking than from all other causes that act specially on the udder. The proper mode of milking is to take the teat in the entire hand, and, after pressing it upward, that it may be well filled from the capacious milk reservoir above, to compress it first at the base between thumb and forefinger, then successively by each of the three succeeding fingers, until completely emptied. The teat is at the same time gently drawn upon, but any severe traction is altogether unnecessary, and highly injurious.

**COWS, TO INCREASE THEIR MILK.**— Give your cows, three times a day, water slightly warm, slightly salted, in which bran has been stirred at the rate of one quart to two gallons of water. You will find, if you have not tried this daily practice, that the cow will give twenty-five per cent more milk, and she will become so much attached to the diet that she will refuse to drink clear water unless very thirsty, but this mess she will drink almost any time and ask for more. The amount of this drink necessary is an ordinary water-pail full each time, morning, noon and night. Avoid giving cows "slops," as they are no more fit for the animal than the human.

**COWS, MILK FEVER IN.**— Immediately there are indications of milk fever, the animal should be restricted to an exclusive hay diet. This treatment should be followed, even in summer time, unless the animal is kept in very close pasture and shows no tendency to fatten. This moderate feeding of hay only should be continued until the fourth or fifth day after calving, at which time the full flow of milk is established, and the danger of puerperal fever has become slight.

**COWS, OLD, WHEN TO KILL.**— It is a question among farmers as to what age cows can be properly used for dairy purposes, and when it is best to dispose of them on account of age. It will depend somewhat on the breed of the animals and the usage they have received. As a general rule, when a cow has entered her teens, she has approximated closely the limit of her usefulness in the dairy line. A good farmer has remarked that a cow was never worn out so long as there was any room on her horns for a new wrinkle.

COWS, SELF-SUCKING.— A good, simple and cheap arrangement to prevent cows from sucking themselves, or each other, may be made by making a halter as follows: Take two or three straps two inches wide, and long enough to reach around the cow's nose. Stitch the edges together, and the ends also, with sharp nails inserted every one and a half-inches, so that the points will stand outward. The heads of the nails should be very large, and should be between the two straps when sewed together. Now fasten two side straps, with a buckle on one end of one, so that when the part with the nails is around the nose the side straps may be buckled together over the head, back of the horns; the part that goes around the nose should be large enough to allow the animal to eat freely. This arrangement will be effectual, but many think it cruel, especially in fly time. A much more desirable and effectual method is to put on a good strong halter, put the animal in a good stall, keep her clean, and feed as much cooked meal as she will eat, until her milking season nearly runs out, and then send her to the butcher. Doing this, it will be found that the milk will pay for the extra feed and care, and the beef will be in prime condition.

COWS, SWELLED BAGS IN.— An excellent remedy for swelled bags of cows, caused by cold, etc., is one-half an ounce of camphor gum to two ounces of sweet oil; pulverize the gum, and dissolve over a slow fire.

COWS' TEATS, WARTS ON.— Warts on the teats of cows usually extend no deeper than the skin. They should not be removed while the cow gives milk. The most effectual way is to take hold of the end of a wart with pliers, and cut it off with sharp shears. The cut should not be deeper than the skin. This remedy will not hurt a cow as much as clipping the skin does sheep when they are being sheared; or a piece of small wire may be twisted around a large wart sufficiently tight to obstruct the circulation of the blood, and left on till the wart drops off, leaving the surface smooth.

CHALK FOR CALVES.— When an animal is found licking his fellow, it is proof that uneasiness is present in the stomach, and the licking of his neighbor is a habit contracted by instinct, with a view of removing the unpleasantness. Unfortunately instinct is not at all times sufficient to avoid dangerous practices, and, if we take for granted that the stomach is at all times fully charged with acrid matter, we shall without hesitation find a remedy. It is only necessary to place within their reach shallow troughs, in which is kept a supply of common chalk. If an animal has a superabundance of acrid secretion, it will most certainly swallow some of the chalk which will as certainly neutralize the excess of acrid. If an animal has not acrid in excess, and partakes of the chalk, it will do no harm. It is often too late to administer remedies to young stock, and the placing of chalk within their reach cannot be made too early.

Cooking Food for Stock.—The great profit of steaming food to feed to stock is, that it converts much of the woody fibre of hay, straw, etc., into soluble, fat-forming nutriments. It is commonly supposed that, as cattle chew the cud, all the nutriment is extracted from the hay, fodder, grain, etc., eaten. So far from this, nothing short of boiling or its equivalent, steaming, can convert woody fibre into soluble nutriment. The same rule is applicable to grain, potatoes, and roots generally; heat is essential to dissolving the starch of grains and roots to render it available, as well as to dissolve the elements out of woody fibre. The heat of the animal system, together with the gastric juices, perform, but imperfectly, the same that steaming or cooking does. Experience and careful experiments have demonstrated that a very much larger proportion of food is assimilated into the system if cooked than if fed uncooked. In very cold weather a greater amount of heat-forming matter is required to keep up animal heat than in mild or warm weather. At such times extra hay or straw may be fed, to sustain this heat, without cutting and steaming, yet this latter process would add largely to its nutriment, without diminishing its heat-forming power. In this connection the following directions will be found serviceable: *To Cook Hay.*—Cut it, wet it well, put it in upright tanks or casks, with false bottom and tight cover, press it down firmly, pass the steam in under the false bottom, and cook until done. *To Cook Corn.*—Soak as many barrels, half full, as you wish to cook, from fifteen to twenty-four hours; turn on steam and cook until done, when the barrels should be full. *To Make Mush.*—Fill as many barrels half-full of water as you wish to make barrels of mush; bring the water nearly to a boil by passing the steam to the bottom; stir in each barrel from one and a half to one and three-fourths bushels of meal until well mixed; then cook until done, when the barrels should be full. *To Cook Vegetables.*—Fill the barrels full, and, if no other cover is at hand, chop the top fine with a shovel; then cover them over with bran meal or provender, and cook until done; have holes in the bottoms of the barrels to carry off condensed steam.

COTTON SEED FOR STOCK.— Very many farmers believe that cotton seed for stock is superior to corn, and ample experiment seems to confirm this view. To cook cotton seed, take a large kettle, which holds from five to six bushels, set it upon a brick furnace, fill it with cotton seed fresh from the gin, and then fill up the kettle with water, and boil something less than one-half an hour; then empty the seed into troughs, and let the cattle and hogs to them. The milk and butter have none of that cotton-seed taste which the green or uncooked seed gives. Both cattle and hogs will keep in good order winter and summer on seed thus prepared; and when you are ready to fatten pork, you have only to add an equal quantity of cotton-seed and corn, and boil as above. Experience has proved that it will fatten much sooner and be equally good as when fattened on corn alone. Your cows will give an abundance of milk all winter when fed in this manner, with but one bushel of corn to four of cotton-seed.

CONDIMENTAL FOOD, THORLEY'S.— The advertisements of patentees of this English preparation would lead to the belief that their "cattle food" contains more real nourishment than the ordinary kinds of food which have hitherto been given; but chemical analysis shows the incorrectness of these statements. There is no secret in the composition, for the test is at hand in a simple analysis. The following is an ordinary formula to make one ton of the meal: Take of Indian meal nine hundred weight, locust bean finely ground six hundred weight, best linseed cake three hundred weight, powdered tumeric and sulphur of each forty pounds, saltpetre twenty pounds, licorice twenty-seven pounds, ginger three pounds, aniseed four pounds, coriander and gentian of each ten pounds, cream of tartar two pounds, carbonate of soda and levigated antimony each six pounds, common salt thirty pounds, Peruvian bark four pounds, fenugreek twenty-two pounds. The reader will observe that the chief ingredients are corn meal, locust bean, and linseed cake; these form its bulk, and constitute nine-tenths of the whole, the remainder being made up of "condiments." There can be no doubt whatever that the nutritive materials which the compound contains are purchased at an enormous expense, and really does not pay for the purchase.

CALVES, CARE OF.— To raise good calves — those that will make good cows — they must be well fed from their birth, as it is impossible to stint a calf in food till one year — or more — old, and then bring the animal into as good condition, in all respects, as could be done if the animal had been well fed. Allow the calf to suck until the milk is fit to use. To learn it to drink, take the calf from the cow at the time mentioned, and fasten it with about six feet of rope in a box stall; then milk the cow, and standing off just far enough for the calf to reach you, wet one finger with milk, put it in its mouth, and gently lower your hand until it is immersed in the milk in the pail; let it continue to have the finger until it has received enough. This is lesson number one. The second lesson is given in this wise: Dip the finger in the milk and place it in its mouth, and when you have brought its mouth in contact with the feed, gradually withdraw your finger and the thing is done. It may be necessary to repeat this at the third time. The secret is that you must stand just far enough so that the calf can just reach the pail of feed, as the rope will then be taut, and hence he cannot reach you, or butt over and spill his milk or feed. It may be remarked in this connection, that calves will thrive better on milk that is not rich in butter than on what is commonly called very rich milk. The nutritive elements of milk reside chiefly in the casein. If you have a cow that gives particularly rich milk, and one that gives a quality poorer in butter, it is better in every way to feed the calf on the milk of the latter. The calf will thrive better, and you get more butter from the milk of the first cow.

CALVES, LICE AND VERMIN ON. — The best applications to destroy lice, nits, etc., is a thorough application of kerosene oil. It is much better than ointment of any kind.

CALVES, TO CURE SCOURS IN. — Take one pint of red-oak acorns, break the shells, and steep thoroughly in three pints of water, and you will have one quart of tea. Give one pint of the same, warm, for the first dose, and the remainder twelve hours after, if necessary. I never knew more than two doses required to effect a cure.

HOLLOW HORN, OR HORN AIL. — This disorder usually attacks cattle in the spring, after a severe winter; likewise those that are in very poor flesh, or those that have been overworked and exposed to severe storms, or reduced by any other diseases, are predisposed to take it. The symptoms are as follows: Eyes dull, discharging yellow matter, dizziness, loss of appetite, shaking of the head, bloody urine, coldness of the horns, stupidity and great debility. The remedies that are recommended are as numerous as they are contradictory. One authority advises boring gimlet holes in the horns three inches from the head, while another advises not to bore at all; one advises to bleed in the neck in the same manner as a horse is bled, while another deprecates bleeding. Another advises to put a mixture of strong vinegar (one-half a teaspoonful), fine salt and ground black pepper (of each a tablespoonful), and, after allowing it to stand over night, to put a tablespoonful in each ear of the animal affected. Another advises the cutting of the hair off the top of the head, and then pour or rub strong spirits of camphor thereon. And still another advises the pouring of the camphor in the ears. Where so many remedies and so much advice is offered, it is to say that not much is known of the real nature of the disease.

PIGS, HOW TO SELECT GOOD.— The desirable points in a good pig are: Sufficient depth and length of body to insure suitable lateral expansion; broad on the loin and breast. The bones small and joints fine; legs no longer than, when fully fat, to just prevent the animal's belly from trailing on the ground when walking; feet firm and sound; the toes to press straightly on the ground and lie well together; the claws should be healthy, upright and even. The head small, the snout short, forehead somewhat convex and curving upward; the ears small but pendulous, somewhat inclined forward; light and thin. His carriage should be lively, sprightly rather than dull and heavy; a lively bright eye, and he should carry his head up rather than down. Those colors which are characteristic of the best breed are to be chosen. The thinner the hair of a black pig the nearer allied it is to the Neapolitan, and consequently the less hardy, either to endure the cold and change of seasons, or to resist disease. White color indicates a connection with the Chinese. Mixed colors show marks of particular breeds; thus, if light or sandy, or red with black marks, the Berkshire blood is detected, etc.

RINGS, BULL, TO INSERT. — This can be done in three ways: 1. By burning the hole through with a pointed rod of iron heated in the forge, thus piercing and searing the wound at the same time. 2. By punching out the hole with an instrument like a leather punch of large size. 3. By piercing the gristle of the nose with a steel-tipped rod (cold), of which the point is formed with two cutting edges. Perhaps it may be an improvement to make the section of the end, just above the point, triangular, or in the shape of a four-pointed star. This last mode is said to be the preferable one. A point of iron about three inches long, and hollowed out at the large end, like the barrel of a key, to receive the round end of the open ring, is used after the hole has been pierced, as a guide to the ring.